Totally Bound Publishing books by Aurora Russell

Single Books
The Au Pair and the Beast

Anywhere and Always
Falling for the Tycoon
Snowbound with the Billionaire

I0670606

Anywhere and Always

SNOWBOUND WITH THE BILLIONAIRE

AURORA RUSSELL

Snowbound with the Billionaire
ISBN # 978-1-83943-960-5
©Copyright Aurora Russell 2021
Cover Art by Erin Dameron-Hill ©Copyright March 2021
Interior text design by Claire Siemaszkiewicz
Totally Bound Publishing

SNOWBOUND WITH THE BILLIONAIRE

Dedication

First, this is dedicated to my own grumpy wizard in a tower and our two sons. You are the lights of my life and make me laugh every day. This is also dedicated to my wonderfully supportive family and friends. To my dad and stepmom, it means the world that you always believe in me. To my brother and sister-in-law, thank you for the encouragement and the tea — both were very effective! Also, this book is dedicated to everyone who pushes through truly rotten times to get to the joy and love waiting on the other side.

Chapter One

Three months earlier

"Don't worry, Rina! You're going to love Rémy's family. His brothers and sister totally can't wait to meet you! Also, you look amazing in that dress." Annelise turned her head halfway to look behind them and Marina wondered what had caught her best friend's attention in the quiet valet area of the sparkling-clean parking garage.

"In fact," Annelise continued in a lower voice, "the back looks pretty freaking fantastic. Are you wearing those butt-boosting underwear things? Or have you been hitting the gym harder than usual?" A spark of mischief lit her eyes before she went on. "I don't mean to be crass…" Annelise waggled her eyebrows.

"Oh, I *know* I've got really nice ass!" Marina had to stifle an undignified snort-laugh as she finished one of their favorite sayings, trying to keep her voice down. "Annelise! Such language so close to the hallowed halls of the Mount Valder Club! I would expect that kind of comment from me, but from you?" Marina mock-chided, but Annelise's light comment had cut the tension and her anxiety in half.

Annelise flushed pink. "Rémy says it isn't as stuffy as its reputation would suggest." She waved her hand dismissively, making the subtle mauve polish that Marina had painted onto her nails a couple of days earlier during a rare girls' night flash in the soft lighting. "And anyway, it's not like anyone is going to dare complain about us. Pierre fast-tracked membership for the whole family as soon as they decided to open a Gaspard Industries branch here in Boston, and we have the entire ballroom reserved just for our soiree tonight. All that must have cost, like, a squillion dollars."

They fell into step together, linking arms by unspoken mutual consent as they headed toward the elevators.

Marina arched one eyebrow. "Look at you, huh? Engaged to a member of one of Canada's most preeminent families—oh, and wealthiest and best-looking, too—for a little over a month and suddenly even the Mount Valder is small potatoes," she teased, and Annelise's cheeks flushed a deeper shade of rose.

"Well, we *have* been going to a lot of parties—all kinds of parties. The lifestyle Rémy has—really, that they all have—to maintain is kind of crazy. And the events are all so fancy and exclusive and luxurious... I'm getting"—she paused thoughtfully as they stepped into the elevator—"not jaded, but definitely a little less impressed by everything than I used to be."

Marina showed surprise. "Really? That's saying something, Anna, for someone who literally plans fancy events for a living."

Annelise shrugged a little sheepishly, the movement making her shimmery golden dress sparkle all around her. "It's crazy, right? But I can see why Rémy avoided a lot of this for so long. I don't know how Pierre does it. He's in the spotlight the most of all of them, since he's the CEO and everything." Annelise leaned closer and Marina smelled the warm vanilla scent her best friend had always favored. "Honestly, I think all of Rémy's siblings would prefer to be at home most nights, but there are such *expectations*... They don't always have a choice."

Annelise had hinted before at the fact that everything might not be as picture-perfect and easy as it seemed for Rémy's fabulously wealthy and powerful family. Case in point, just a few months earlier, the Gaspard siblings had had a crazy ex-friend — also the ex-fiancé of Rémy's sister — who'd ended up trying, repeatedly, to murder them. He was still awaiting trial.

"That does make sense," Marina agreed, nodding slowly. She thought of how she and Annelise had been struggling over the past months to make time to get together even once every couple of weeks. Marina totally understood that Anna had been caught up in not only the intensity of a new romance but also in being introduced as a member of 'the Gaspard family'. Marina wasn't offended — *of course I'm not* — but she *missed* Annelise. Plus, not meeting her best friend for lunch or drinks as often anymore had made her own small studio apartment seem so much emptier.

That was part of what had made Annelise's invitation to tonight's party so important — so much so that Marina had gotten a little uncharacteristically nervous. It was a small, exclusive event only for close friends and contacts of the Gaspards and also an unofficial celebration of Rémy's oldest brother, Pierre's, expected reentry into society. Marina wasn't sure what had been going on, and Annelise had been maddeningly vague, but Pierre had been letting everyone else shoulder the lion's share of the family obligations for months while he mysteriously wasn't around. Personally, her guess was that he had been hanging out on the family yacht off the coast of St. Tropez with a revolving door of supermodels. Whatever the reason, he was finally deigning to come back at tonight's event.

At that thought, Marina's previous anxiety started to ramp up again, but she took a deep breath and straightened her spine. *I am smart, fun, beautiful and Annelise's best friend*, she reminded herself. *This is for Anna, and if they don't like me or think I'm good enough, it won't be because I haven't given it my damnedest.* As though feeling her tension, Annelise squeezed her hand reassuringly as they walked toward the brightly lit ballroom with unmistakable party sounds coming from it, and Marina raised her chin with a confidence that she wasn't sure she totally felt. It was showtime.

Two hours later, Marina was shocked to find that she was actually having fun. Clothilde, Annelise's future sister-in-law, was kind, down-to-earth and had a wickedly sharp wit that made her feel like an instant friend, in spite of the fact that she looked like she should be on the cover of a high-fashion magazine. Actually, Marina seemed to recall that Clothilde *had* been on the cover of several women's magazines in the past. Luc, who was Rémy's younger brother, had flown in from Paris just for the event and he was absolutely charming, but in a genuine way. He was handsome, funny and his light flirtation had made her giggle and blush.

Still, so much dancing and socializing had worn her down a little bit, so when Rémy had asked Annelise to dance again for the umpteenth time that evening, leaving Marina alone for a moment, she had seized her chance to sneak away and rest her feet. Not that she was ungrateful — no, it gave her warm fuzzies to think of how attentive Rémy and his family had been to her all evening, obviously determined not to let her feel awkward or nervous for a second — but she was just a little overwhelmed. This was Annelise's scene, not hers, and her cheeks were starting to hurt from smiling as much as her feet were beginning to ache from spending too long in high heels.

She ducked into the dark hallway behind the ballroom and noticed that the rooms were labeled with the names of prominent Bostonians from the past. They looked like conference rooms, and she nearly sighed with relief. No one was likely to be having a conference at this time of the evening, so she could take a little break in peace to pull herself together again. She opened the first heavy, dark-wood door, which was surprisingly well-oiled and silent. Even with the lights out, she could make out the outlines of several chairs surrounding an enormous table. *Definitely a conference room. Perfect.*

She pulled the door closed behind her and let out a long sigh, stepping out of her shoes immediately and relishing the feel of the cool hardwood floor underneath her stockinged feet. If she were honest with herself, it wasn't just the physical strain of the party she'd wanted to escape. It was also the brilliant, effervescent happiness and love that she had felt radiating from Annelise and Rémy. She was overjoyed for her best friend — *absolutely, I am* — but here in the darkness, alone, she could admit that she was envious, too. The hole that remained in her soul, the slash of pain whenever she remembered the beautiful, wonderful man she'd loved and with whom she'd planned an entire lifetime of happiness, ached and throbbed more than any physical wound ever could. *Oh, Jaime.*

She could picture his face vividly, although now, after so much time, she hated that he was starting to look more and more like the pictures she had of him and less like the man in her memories. He had been young—*so incredibly young*. She'd been cheated by a stray bullet, friendly fire during a skirmish, out of knowing what he would look like any older than twenty-one. What would he have looked like if he were as old as the woman she saw in her own reflection these days? Would he even recognize her, dancing in a ballroom with multiple men in tailored suits, sipping champagne and eating foie-gras and caviar canapes from silver platters, offered by tastefully dressed and silent waitstaff? Joking and flirting with Annelise's future brother-in-law as well as several of the other charming older men who were friends of Rémy's family?

That was the crux of her tiredness…the reason she'd needed to escape. What the hell was she doing, enjoying herself like this when Jaime was cold and buried in the Virginia ground, still wearing his dress blues? And when she'd sent him away the way she had… But she refused to even start to think about that tonight. She tried not to cry anymore, and most days, she succeeded. But this evening, watching Annelise with her fiancé, wrapped up in his love at every moment, had made Marina feel fragile all over again. As if Jaime's loss were closer tonight, somehow.

She felt for and made contact with the closest chair, planning to sink down onto it.

"Unless you want to find yourself on my lap—which I'm not opposed to, mind you—you'd better choose another seat, *chérie*."

Marina yelped and leapt away, her heart pounding up into her throat. The man's voice had been deep, raspy and amused, and she might have found it sexy under other circumstances. However, alone in a dark conference room behind doors that had looked extremely thick was not the right circumstance for anything but terror.

"Why didn't you say anything when I came in?" she finally managed to ask, wincing at the accusation in her tone. She heard a rustle and could almost feel his shrug.

"I hoped that you would leave quickly, and I didn't want to startle you," he answered simply.

His answer made sense, but Marina was irrationally annoyed. "What are you doing in here, anyway? Who would leave a party to come sit in the dark?"

His chuckle was dry, and goosebumps raised on her arms. "Who indeed?"

She pursed her lips. "*Touché*," she acknowledged.

"I'll reveal some of my demons if you show me yours." His tone was mocking as he echoed the childish dare. She couldn't help the way her pulse quickened, as though he were offering to show her something illicit.

"No thank you." She winced at how prim her tone was, but the stranger's amused chuckle rolled through the small room.

"I didn't think you would, but I hoped…" He trailed off meaningfully.

"I'm going to sit down in, uh, another chair," she announced, trying to change the subject. "My feet are killing me from so much dancing."

"Be my guest, *chérie*. Seat yourself anywhere you desire." Again, his rough voice made his words sound like innuendo. She sank down onto the chair one over from his. "I can imagine your lovely feet must throb from those beautiful yet completely impractical shoes you wore earlier. I could rub them, if you'd like?"

"*What?* Of course not!" Marina gasped, actually shocked at his audacity. "You can't just…offer to massage a complete stranger!"

"Good point," he answered in a reasonable tone. "Tell me a few things about yourself so I can offer again."

She laughed in spite of herself.

His chair creaked as he leaned forward. She could make out his silhouette now that her eyes had adjusted, and from his frame, he looked to be very tall and muscular. A dark, spicy scent teased her nose, masculine and exotic.

"Here's an easy question. Why did you leave the party? The Gaspards always throw the best… It's expected."

It might have been the shroud of darkness that caused her to pay such close attention to his voice, or maybe she was just attuned to him, but there was a curious tension in his tone.

"Apart from my feet starting to ache? I…had to get away from all the happiness for a bit. My best friend is engaged to one of the Gaspards—Rémy—and they're blissfully in love." As soon as the words left her mouth, Marina couldn't believe she'd actually said them out loud—and to a near-stranger no less.

The man made a sound of understanding. "Ah, of course. And you love him, too?" There was a resigned sadness in his voice.

"What? *No!*" Marina denied instantly. "I mean, he's great, and wonderful for Annelise, wonderful *to* her, but…no. I just—" She trailed off, not wanting to tell him about Jaime, not wanting to sound like the totally bitchy, selfish friend she knew she was being.

"You don't like the Gaspards, then? It is common. They are notorious as well as famous."

Marina noticed the stranger's accent more on those words. He was obviously one of the French-Canadian guests, which wasn't surprising, since they made up the majority of the party.

"I like the Gaspards. Or, at least, I think Rémy is awesome, and even though I just met his brother and sister, Luc and Clothilde, tonight, they seem great too. I'm not sure about the older brother, Pierre. I hear he can be a cold bastard." She gasped again as she realized she'd been bashing one of the Gaspards to someone who was probably friends with all of them. "I mean, that's the rumor, but…like I said, I've never met him, so I don't really know," she finished lamely.

Luckily, her companion didn't seem offended. "The rumors are correct. Pierre Gaspard can be utterly ruthless when it comes to his siblings and their associates."

Marina was so relieved that she didn't pick up on a subtle warning in his tone.

"What matters is that your friend is happy, though, is it not? She must love the lifestyle her fiancé can provide for her."

"Yes, she does. It's like a fairy tale, isn't it? And Annelise is the princess. She always loved pretending we were in a fairy tale when we were kids. I mean, nothing is perfect." Marina thought of how Annelise had admitted that the lifestyle of being a Gaspard was filled with obligations. "But I'm sure they won't be so busy handling so many public appearances and duties once Pierre gets back from wherever he's been. Annelise and Rémy just want a little more time to enjoy each other." She broke off suddenly, embarrassed again at how much she'd revealed. God, Annelise was going to kill her. She'd been babbling away into the darkness, and she knew part of it was nervousness, but also...the stranger just felt so easy to talk to.

"Ah, yes, the roaming Pierre. Tell me... What do Annelise and Rémy have to say about his whereabouts?" The question was probing. Marina ignored her growing sense of unease, which was buried by her curiosity. Maybe this stranger, who must be close to the Gaspard family, could finally give her more information about where the hell the oldest Gaspard brother had been.

"That's the weird part. They don't really have anything to say, but...I think they're covering for something."

"Oh yes?" her companion prompted gently.

Marina nodded, even though she knew her mysterious fellow guest would barely be able to see the gesture. "I suppose it could be something like he's been sick—or maybe he's an alcoholic or drug addict in rehab," she speculated, really warming to the topic. "But my best guess is that he's been living it up on one of their yachts, hooking up with supermodels and too busy partying to take care of his responsibilities."

There was a long silence that stretched uncomfortably in the darkened room.

"Ms. Lopez," he began, and Marina felt herself go cold at his use of her name, "I realize that you are new to this world and this level of society, and I am willing to make concessions to your ignorance. However, even *you* should be aware that as someone closely connected to my future sister-in-law, what you say might very well reflect back on my family."

Marina felt like she was back in her family's cozy little home, eight years old again, and being lectured by her nana, who'd just told her that she was disappointed and had expected better of her young granddaughter. She shifted uncomfortably in her seat.

"You should know better," the stranger continued, "than to speculate on where I have been and what I have been doing. If you can't control your tongue and prevent it from gossiping, I will be forced to take countermeasures. Do you think you can manage never to gossip about my family again, especially to a stranger who very well could have been a reporter who'd be only too happy to print your comments as truth?"

Marina felt sick as the realization of who the stranger was dawned on her. The flighty, rich playboy she'd been talking about didn't seem to be very flighty at all, and he was sitting right next to her.

"I apologize for my comments," she said, feeling the heat of a blush creep up into her cheeks and continuing all the way out to her chest and even her arms. "I don't normally speculate so much or say things like that to strangers, but… There's no excuse. I didn't think of the implications. I *will* be more careful in the future."

Pierre rose, even taller and more imposing than she'd realized.

"I hope that you will." His voice grew colder as he leaned over her chair. "I will do anything…*anything at all*…to protect my family's reputation." Marina thought he was finished, but he continued, surprising her. "Not because it is so precious to me, personally, but because it affects the welfare of thousands of employees who depend on us — on *me* — and who could be harmed by negative rumors."

"I understand," Marina answered, and she realized that she did. While she had focused on how much fun it must be to have so much wealth and power, their company and influence must also be a burden to manage.

"Good." The word was clipped, and he sounded…disappointed? "Now, will you allow me to escort you to your vehicle?"

Dios, Marina thought. *I'm being kicked out politely but firmly. If I don't leave, is he going to call a bouncer? Does a social club even have bouncers, or does he bring his own?* She stiffened her spine and rose with as much pride as she could muster while barefoot in a dark room.

"No, thank you. I can find my own way, *Monsieur* Gaspard." She slipped her shoes back on at the door and made an intensely dignified exit.

As the door closed behind her, she thought she heard him whisper, "Too bad."

Chapter Two

Present

"You are so incredibly sweet to get started setting everything up without us!"

Even with the bad connection, made even scratchier by coming through the massive SUV's Bluetooth speakers, Marina heard the real gratitude and affection in Annelise's voice.

"Yeah, no. You know I'm never sweet, Anna! Too much pepper in me, I think. But I want to do this for you…for you and Rémy. Your engagement is really something special to celebrate!" She paused and added, "What was I going to do instead, anyway? Stay late at work and listen to The Dragon complain for an extra three hours, then get Chinese take-out and ice cream on the way home to watch Netflix all night in my empty apartment?"

"When you put it that way…"

Marina wasn't sure if Annelise had trailed off for emphasis or if the line had cut out. Her suspicion that it was the line was realized when her friend came back mid-sentence.

"...know you don't like him but he's really not so bad."

Marina groaned. "I lost you for a second, hon. But if you're trying to set me up again with that nice analyst from Rémy's new office, just...don't, okay? He's hot and funny and perfect...for someone else. Just not me."

"He *is* super nice, isn't he? Colton, like one of those country singers you secretly love to listen to but almost never admit to liking. But that's not who I was talking about...although you seriously *do* need to pay attention to your nonexistent love life."

Annelise's tone was light, but Marina felt an unexpected jab to somewhere underneath her ribs, curiously close to her heart.

"Not nonexistent, Anna. I'm just... I guess I'm still not ready."

Annelise's voice was instantly contrite. "Rina, I'm sorry. I didn't mean to make you sad. I'm really trying not to push."

Marina shook her head and smiled reassuringly at the car display, as if Annelise could see her. "And I appreciate that, especially since I know that the thing you want most in this world now, apart from world peace and those shoes from the Louboutin window display on Newbury Street, is to see everyone around you as brimming with joy as you and Rémy are."

Her friend's laugh, full and silvery, was always infectious, and Marina couldn't help but smile as she heard it again now.

"I guess I am still a little, uh, love crazed?"

Marina raised one eyebrow. "Oh, is *that* what they're calling it these days?"

Annelise guffawed. "Rina! I'll have you know that I like Rémy all the time, not just in bed."

"Um, *yeah*, your neighbor mentioned that to me five or six times when I came over to feed Ms. Penelope when you and Rémy were in Paris two weeks ago. You know, you really should try to use that thing called a door. They make them nowadays with locks and everything. You could have given him a heart attack. His words, not mine."

Annelise snorted. "Okay, fair point that we could have been more discreet that one time. *One time*. But Mr. Mundy would have died happy. I swear, he's the biggest gossip in Boston…like the Neighborhood Watch meets the old ladies who used to sit in the front window of the teahouse in our hometown, but on steroids. Does he *never* sleep?"

Marina could hear the smile in Annelise's voice, underlaid with a kind of affectionate exasperation.

"You distracted me, though! I wasn't talking about Colton or Mr. Mundy or…" The static was suddenly loud in the silence of the SUV cab.

"Anna! You're breaking up! Can you hear me?" Marina shouted and waved her hand, feeling silly.

"Just found out…had to warn you… Don't get mad… Be nice."

Now, when she could hear it at all, Annelise's voice sounded tinny and like it was coming from a submarine at the bottom of the ocean instead of from Rémy's family's fabulous estate-compound in Montreal, surrounded by cell towers.

"Had to warn me about *what*? *Who*? *Anna*!" She pressed the buttons on the screen, but instead of getting her friend back, the line beeped then cut out entirely. Marina pressed the button to call Anna back three times, but she might have been pressing on a plank of wood for all the good it did. Her reception was totally gone. She made a sound of disgust and blew out a frustrated breath, making the little wispy hairs around her face that had fallen from her messy updo tickle her cheeks.

"Damn Vermont. I hate surprises," she said out loud…to herself. Well, and the approximately five million pine and other snow-covered trees that surrounded her. While she'd been on the phone with Annelise, Marina realized she'd passed distinctly out of the realm of anything resembling civilization into straight-up Boondocklandia. *Boondocklandia, Vermont is probably a really hot fall destination for leaf peepers*, Marina thought to herself wryly. *I bet I couldn't even get a hotel reservation on my budget.*

Of course, now, in the late winter, off the beaten path to the main ski mountains, she basically had the road to herself—which was a good thing, considering that the pretty little snowflakes that had started to dust the black hood of the extravagantly oversized SUV that Anna and Rémy had insisted that she borrow were now becoming a thick, swirling mass, blanketing the already snow-covered mountains around her. She turned on the radio, pressing and holding the seek button to find some sort of weather report. The first station was classical, the second station was in French—*French! How freaking close to Canada am I now?*—and the third and final station was a little staticky, but a whole lot country. She recognized the song, one of her favorites, about a smoky bar and honky-tonk dancing. She had never quite figured out what honky-tonk meant, but good Lord, she *loved* that word.

Annelise was right about her secret love of country music. She hadn't grown up listening to it, but after Jaime had died, every song had made her so sad.

Everything they'd listened to together, which had been...*everything*, had just made her heart hurt. Well, except country and polka. Still, she loved music. And so, faced with the choice of either giving it up or making a radical change, she had taken the plunge into one hundred percent American country music. And man, oh, man, she couldn't believe how much she'd been missing!

She sang along for a minute, hoping they'd interrupt eventually with a weather forecast, slowing down almost unconsciously as the fluffy snow came toward her windshield like confetti made of downy feathers. She got her wish at the end of the song, but what she heard wasn't good.

"Be careful out there, folks. From the Kingdom to the mountains, cooling temperatures mean the snow today is going to be heavier than originally predicted. Most of us are going to see snowfall totals in the twelve- to eighteen-inch range, but there are now going to be pockets of up to twenty-four inches or more. If you're on the road, get somewhere safe, but by the weekend, we should be enjoying some seriously sweet, fresh powder. And now, here's the latest from Kendina Hager..."

As her SUV kept climbing, the radio station cut out before Marina could hear what that latest song might be. She blew another frustrated breath upward, thinking that she should count herself lucky that she'd heard a forecast at all, pressing the button to turn the radio off entirely. Twelve to eighteen inches of snow, with pockets of up to twenty-four inches or more, was a heck of a lot of snow on top of the over a foot that was already blanketing the ground. They could get a decent amount of the white stuff where she lived in Boston, but this was...outside her comfort zone. She bit her lip and looked worriedly out at the enormous flakes whizzing by the car, some of which were now building up on the hood before they melted with the heat and slid off.

She was a little comforted when she saw a pair of headlights following her at a small distance so she could barely make them out. "At least I'm not the only person crazy enough to be out in this weather," she muttered under her breath. In fact, she realized she had seen dim lights behind her several times now, and as the vehicle behind her started to creep closer, she felt the oddest trickle of unease down her spine. The fantastical notion that maybe she was being followed crept in. Then the car turned off on a side-road and she told herself the snow was making her a little crazy. Alone on the road, dark as evening in the middle of the day, it did feel a little eerie. She nearly jumped out of her seat, saved only by her seatbelt, when the loud mechanical female voice rang out in the car.

"*In point-five miles, turn left.*" Incongruously, the voice had a clipped British accent. Still, making a turn off this smaller highway must mean that she was at least getting close. In fact, if the estimated arrival time on the built-in GPS was correct, she should reach her destination in about twenty minutes. Marina heaved an inward sigh of relief. The roads were really getting coated in snow now, and she'd feel much better once she arrived at the remodeled mountain estate that Rémy's family owned. They called it a lodge, but from the pictures she'd seen, it looked like some sort of magnificent Victorian-castle-take on Adirondack chic. Or rather, Green Mountain chic, she supposed, since Vermont was the Green Mountain State. *White mountain state today, guys*, Marina thought to herself with a dry laugh.

Annelise had sent Marina pictures of Beauxrêves Lodge when she and Rémy had decided to hold their engagement party there, and the place looked seriously spectacular. Marina had become even more familiar with it as she'd helped Annelise plan and organize. Annelise said that they could have hired lots of events people, but she'd wanted to plan it mostly herself. Of course, the wedding plans and Rémy's business trips had taken up more time than she'd realized, and Marina had been happy to step in as well.

She'd worked with Bonnie and George, the caretakers who also arranged for outside assistance when there were guests, and they'd assured her that all of the decorations would be onsite today, along with plenty of staff. The caterers were scheduled for tomorrow. Annelise had a 'winter wonderland meets uptown glam' vision for the engagement party, one which Marina had been enthusiastically onboard with. She wasn't sure if Rémy cared one way or the other. When they'd discussed it over cocktails one night after Marina and Annelise had had an afternoon gab mixed with planning session, he'd just smiled, looked down at his fiancée with soft eyes and said that whatever made Annelise happy would make him happy. Underneath the warm glow Marina had for her closest friend, she'd also experienced another twinge of unmistakable envy. She *knew* she was a terrible person. She'd thrown herself even more enthusiastically into party planning.

Now, of course, Marina worried about the outside help that was supposed to be coming the next day. Would they be able to make it there? Was it even safe for them to be there, if they were? Looking around, it was hard to believe that they might realistically have any sort of party tomorrow, no matter how intimate it was supposed to be. Annelise and Rémy would understand. Marina wasn't worried about that. Annelise would for sure call Eduardo, Marina's brother, if Marina wasn't able to for any reason. And her nana hadn't felt up to making the trip, so they were going to have a fancy dinner when they returned. Rémy had already reserved a private room at an elegant restaurant very close to the exorbitantly priced but truly lovely assisted living facility that she and Eduardo worked extremely hard to pay for each month. Come to think of it, Marina thought that Rémy's family and close friends would be understanding, too. Or at least she knew that Luc and Clothilde and the other friends she'd met at the party three months earlier would be, with one glaring exception.

Pierre. Marina gritted her teeth as she thought about him. He would probably be furious that Mother Nature dared to imagine that she had power over the mighty Gaspard family. Rémy had invited her to two family dinners since that infamous party — well, infamous only in *her* mind, since she'd never breathed a word of what had happened between herself and Pierre to Annelise — but Pierre had cancelled at the last minute for both. She ought to have been grateful that she hadn't had to see him, but instead she'd been illogically disappointed. She was embarrassed in a way that made all her insides squirm at the memory of what she'd said and how he'd interpreted it in the worst possible light, but before everything had gone wrong, she'd felt...*something.* Some spark of excitement that she hadn't felt in a long time.

After their encounter, she'd looked up pictures of the eldest Gaspard brother, since she hadn't gotten a good look in the low lighting, and *wowzah*, the man was smoking hot...like a Roman god, complete with a pronounced nose, dark hair and even darker eyes, and muscles on top of muscles. But she thought his eyes looked distant in all the pictures, except when he was with his family.

Even though she hadn't given her the full story, Marina knew she must not have a done a great job hiding her strong feelings about Pierre with Annelise, because Anna had called her on it almost immediately. Unfortunately, Annelise had assumed that Pierre had been rude or gruff and made Marina uncomfortable, just through some sort of misunderstanding. Marina hadn't had the heart to correct her friend, since the truth made her look so damn bad, although she thought she'd at least successfully stopped her best friend from talking to Pierre about it. Part of Marina actually hoped that maybe the snowstorm had affected his precious schedule and he might no longer be able to attend, but then she chided herself for the thought. That would make Rémy and Annelise unhappy, which was not okay, so she would smile her way through any and all future meetings with Pierre, no matter how uncomfortable he made her. She sighed, the sound loud in spite of the rhythmic click-clack of the windshield wipers that couldn't quite keep up with removing the thick snowflakes from the glass. "What a waste of an otherwise perfect specimen of manhood," she said out loud.

Alone, she could acknowledge that, in spite of her waking dislike of Pierre, her sleeping subconscious certainly didn't have the same scruples. She'd had more than one spicy—no, downright sexy—dream about the eldest Gaspard brother—dreams that had left her hot and aching. Even now, she shifted on her seat at the memory of the latest one, with him ordering her to kneel, naked while he was fully clothed and unzip his tuxedo pants with her teeth, then…but *no. Uh-uh.* She was *not* going there. Deciding again, as she had before, that the dreams were just a random manifestation of the desires and needs of her body over which she had no control, she shook off the stirring memories of the dreams and refocused on the road.

When she finally pulled onto the non-descript, unmarked road that led to the lodge itself, she was white-knuckled and stiff from holding herself forward and driving slowly and carefully for what had felt like forever, but what the digital display clock on the dash told her had only been about an hour. Still, an hour to go a distance that should have only taken twenty minutes was pretty grueling. *At least I haven't had to deal with Boston traffic this afternoon*, she thought with a wry smile.

The road was narrow but seemed well-maintained and certainly regularly plowed. In spite of that, it was carpeted with a thick blanket of the snow that had been falling rapidly over the past hour, so she had to inch along carefully. She was grateful to be going so slowly, or she would have missed the downed tree in middle of the road entirely, with how restricted the visibility was. As it was, she nearly didn't see it until she was practically on top of the enormous bulk blocking the road, and she slammed on her brakes. For a second, it seemed as if she would stop in time to avoid hitting the massive trunk—and it was absolutely enormous, like some primordial old-growth giant that had probably been there before Columbus had even dreamed of sailing to the Indies—but the snow was slick underneath her tires, and with a squeal followed by a crunching thud, she slid right into it, almost as though she hadn't braked at all.

After her heart stopped trying to jump right out of her chest and she could take a breath without feeling dizzy, she did a mental full-body assessment. *Feet and legs are okay, back is okay, torso, arms, head – all okay.* She thought her neck might be a little stiff, but she was reserving judgment.

"*Gracias a Dios*...thank God, thank *God*," she breathed in both Spanish and English, pausing to feel incredibly grateful that she seemed uninjured. Unlike the beautiful, top-of-the line luxury SUV, the hood of which had crumpled a bit so that it was tented in front of her. She pressed the button that should start the ignition, but she only heard a loud *click click click* with no sign of the engine turning over. "Shit, shit, shit, shit!" she continued out loud. "Lickity, plickity, dickity, frick!" she added, using something she and Annelise had come up with when trying to be more ladylike and avoid swearing. But *damn it*, she felt terrible about destroying – or at least badly damaging – something that Annelise had so kindly loaned to her.

She sat there for a long moment, considering her options. There was no point in calling anyone for the car now, with the storm raging, and she had zero bars of reception on her cell phone anyway. Right before she'd run into the tree, which must have just come down in the storm since it looked oddly naked, not yet fully covered in heavy snow – unlike everything else around – she thought the GPS had said she was only two-tenths of a mile from her destination. The road was narrow, and it was hard to see with the swirling white flakes, but she'd certainly know if she was in the middle of the thick forest on either side instead of on the road, so she thought she should be safe walking the short distance.

Eyeing her silly leather boots, which had seemed cute and stylish and pretty reasonable for a luxury lodge in Vermont when she'd put them on that morning, she groaned but steeled herself. Her feet would be cold, and the boots would be ruined, although she didn't care about that at this point. She just needed to get to the warmth and shelter of the lodge. However, the thought of stepping out of the limited shelter offered by the SUV into the howling storm was daunting.

Unexpectedly, and in a way that pierced her heart and took the air from her lungs, the memory of Jaime's face popped into her head – tall, handsome, confident and filled with the strength of his convictions about right and wrong, just as he had been the last time she'd seen him. She knew that he would have encouraged her to go for it – would have reassured her that she could do it. She was warmed by the memory, even while tears stung her eyes for an instant as it faded.

She made sure she had everything she needed from the front seat tucked into her pockets, slung her handbag crosswise over her chest, and slipped on her heavy coat, hat, scarf and gloves. At least she'd managed to wear *some* appropriate cold-weather gear, she thought with dark humor. As soon as she opened the car door, a wave of cold engulfed her, along with snowflakes moving so fast that they felt like little ice chips whipping at her cheeks. She slammed the door shut then kept her head down and followed the shiny black metal of the side of the vehicle to the front of the hood. From what she could see, the SUV was pretty banged up, but she hoped it was still fixable. In any case, now that she was right next to it, she realized that there was no way she was going to be able to scramble over the top of the tree trunk, as she'd hoped. But as she turned, she saw that the tree had snapped more fully closer to the other side of the road, and she thought she might be able to get over that part without having to detour into the woods.

Her breath fanned out in cold puffs, which she was surprised she could even see with how thickly the snow was falling, as she moved as quickly as the slippery surface of the road under her totally unsuitable boots would allow, but she made it to the break without falling. As she'd hoped, with some splintering — which she was careful to avoid — this part of the tree trunk was shorter and she could hoist herself up over it after a couple tries, sliding down hard, her arm scraping along the bark, to land with her bottom in the snow. Her knee was twisted a little oddly but seemed okay. She noted the minor pain and cold absently, too elated at being over the tree trunk to muster any deep concern, and set off at a slow, deliberate pace along the road. The sound of the wind and the snow muffled everything else, so that she felt as if she were alone. Alone on the road, sure, but also alone in the world. It was disconcerting, and she was uncomfortable that she found it so unsettling. She was a strong, self-reliant woman, and she liked her own company. So why was she so unhappy to be forced to confront her own thoughts? And did it matter, when she would freeze to death if she didn't get to the cabin?

She tried to speed her pace from snail to turtle, without much success, but finally — *finally!* — the dark shape of a huge cabin loomed. In fact, since she hadn't been able to see it earlier, she was practically on top of it. The pictures hadn't done it justice. Oh, sure, Marina could make out the shapes of the logs that made up the structure, but it was the size of an entire lodge, and she noted with no small measure of relief that a welcoming yellow light shone, even through the thick flakes next to the cheery red door.

Annelise must have told the caretakers I was still on my way, she thought, and sent another quick thank-you to her friend and to the kindly older couple who must have risked getting stuck themselves to ensure she was comfortable. *Quite a change from my usual cold studio apartment*, she thought absently, but squashed the thought as soon as it came. She had a fun, chic little pad, perfect for the small amount of time she was there between working hard and going out with friends.

She trudged more than walked the final few steps to the door, where snow had drifted into a high mound against the frame. The feeling of the front of the cabin was luxurious, but rustic, so the high-tech thumb-pad and keypad were incongruous. *Thank God they don't have a retinal scanner*, she thought, since she was pretty sure her eyelashes had frozen to her cheeks. She fumbled her right hand out of one wool-lined glove and stifled a gasp as the pad of her thumb touched the smooth, icy surface of the reader. The machine blipped and beeped and, with a flash of green light, she heard several bolts unlock.

"Thank goodness!" she breathed, the words puffing away almost as soon as she'd spoken them. "Next...next..." she searched her mind to remember what the nice security guard Annelise had sent over with the SUV had said, since she sure as heck wasn't going to get the piece of paper she'd written everything down on out of the back pocket of her leggings any time soon. Although maybe she should let the alarm go off, she thought a little hysterically, because at least then someone would come to check on her. She doubted even all of the Gaspard fortune and power could overcome tonight's blizzard quickly, though.

"Keypad inside, then back outside," she murmured, recalling the order. She only had time to take in an impression of a beautifully warm and toasty interior, glowing with a soft, burnished light, before she located the keypad on the wall. She quickly typed in the date Jaime had proposed to her, followed by the name of her childhood cat. Another set of beeps followed, along with another light, this time white. She ducked back outside. Marc, that was the name of the security guard and driver who usually stayed with Annelise and Rémy at all times in Boston. Marc had said that it was unexpected, to go inside before going back out. It felt even colder back outside of the shelter of the cabin's entryway, and the wind seemed to blow right through her coat, as if it weren't there. Still, with one frozen finger, this time she typed her nana's birthday, followed by her brother Eduardo's birthday as well.

She waited for the same beeps, which seemed to take way too darn long, but finally a green light flashed and she darted back through the door. Marc's warning echoed in her ear. She had to close the door within thirty seconds or she'd have to repeat the entire process. With that in mind, she slammed the front door behind her with a much louder thump than she'd intended. The sound echoed through the blessedly silent foyer, which seemed even quieter after the constant noise of the storm, but she allowed herself a smile of relief that felt like it almost cracked her frozen cheeks. She'd made it safely, and now she would be warm and cozy in the cabin for at least a little while.

She started to sigh but, as she looked up, the noise turned into a shriek of surprise at the sudden appearance of the tall man in front of her.

At first, she just stared at the intruder with mute horror…but why did he look so familiar? With sudden recognition, her temper flared and she narrowed her eyes. She should have recognized him right away, from all of the nightmares she'd had after her mortifying initial encounter with him. The oldest Gaspard brother, scion of the family, CEO of the family's multi-billion-dollar empire, and general all-around boss of everything and everyone he ever had around him, Pierre Gaspard stood before her—slouched, really, leaning up against the doorframe from the entryway to the spacious living room behind him.

"*You,*" she breathed, furious at how foolish he'd made her feel. "How *dare* you frighten me like that! You could have given me a heart attack, sneaking up on me like a cat!"

His answering chuckle made her want to stamp her foot childishly.

"First, Ms. Lopez...or can I call you Marina?" He held up a hand when she would have answered angrily. "Never mind. Considering the circumstances, I think you should definitely be Marina now, and you can feel free to call me Pierre."

She opened her mouth to speak but was stopped again by the sheer force of his smile. It lit his entire face, making his eyes crinkle at the corners, making him look incongruously younger and more relaxed. Damn, but she hadn't realized how very magnetic he was.

"I did not sneak up on you, like a cat or otherwise. I always move purposefully because I usually have to...to show I'm in control, dominant, supremely confident at all times. You, *chérie*, were making enough noise to wake the dead, going in and out of the house, setting off beeping. I am impressed that you successfully navigated the codes. I assume someone set them for you today as they're reset daily and also keyed in your thumbprint."

She nodded almost in spite of herself. "Marc did. Annelise asked him to."

Pierre inclined his head slightly. "Of course. I saw a message from him but lost reception here before it could download. And so…here we are." His dark eyes seemed to twinkle with some sort of secret amusement, daring her to share it. "I'd like to ask why you're here, but that can wait. The reality is that it doesn't matter, because there's no way either of us can safely leave until the blizzard outside is over and we can dig our way out of the snow."

Marina knew he was probably right, but she hated the way he looked so superior and knowing. So *reasonable*. The last person she wanted to be stuck anywhere with was Pierre-freaking-Gaspard, the Ice Prince himself.

"I'm sure we can call someone for help. There's no need for the two of us to be…*trapped* here, together." She tried to keep her tone just as reasonable as his had been, not to betray how much she didn't want to be stuck anywhere with him, much less in a remote lodge in the Vermont wilderness.

Pierre's face was impassive, but some flicker in his dark eyes told her that she hadn't hidden her emotions very well. "And who would you suggest that we call who would be able to reach us in the storm?"

"I, uh, there must be *someone*. The police and firefighters still respond to emergencies during blizzards," she answered, picturing some very hardy Vermont firefighters coming to get them.

"While I know that you may not find my company pleasant, I hardly think it counts as an emergency, hm? Perhaps we should allow them to use their limited resources to respond to true emergency calls instead? There are usually more than enough of those in a blizzard with people getting stranded, medical issues, and the like."

His gentle rebuff made her feel ashamed.

"Sure. I mean, yes, obviously. Emergency services is a last resort for true emergencies." Her heart sank as she realized the truth of her statement. "There must be some other option, though. Snowmobiles or helicopters…maybe a dogsled?" She knew she was throwing out ideas wildly, but something about Pierre made her incredibly uncomfortable. She had initially felt a kinship with him, then she'd been ashamed by how dirty and unworthy he'd made her feel with his cutting comments — made even harsher by how much she'd originally liked him when she'd thought he was just a smart, funny stranger. She shivered involuntarily, feeling a wet droplet of melted snow trickle down from her hair under her coat and shirt, down her bare back.

"We can certainly discuss other, er, *reasonable* options, but I haven't strayed so far from the good manners my parents taught me as to let you stand here in those wet things."

He stepped closer and suddenly the sodden, cold weight of her coat, hat and scarf felt heavy on her body. He smelled warm and spicy, dark but comforting somehow too.

"Let me help you take your clothes off." His words were low, in that deep, raspy voice, and her body gave an involuntary shiver. Not a cold shiver this time though, but a hot one. She opened her mouth as she gasped and her cheeks heated with a blush.

He quirked up one side of his mouth in a lopsided smile. "I'm sorry," he said in an unrepentant tone. "I get the English words wrong sometimes, you know. Let me help you take your, er, outer things off."

Marina had planned to refuse, but when she raised her eyes to his, she was mesmerized by the intensity of his expression. Holding her gaze, he slowly unwound her scarf, hanging it up on the artistically arrayed silver antler hooks that she hadn't noticed behind her. When his fingers brushed her cheek, which was still flushed as he took off her hat, she jumped at the jolt of pure sensation she felt where his skin touched hers. She backed up with a small cry and took her coat off herself, then bent over to unlace her ruined boots.

She didn't look up again until she'd put them under the hooks and stood in her stocking feet. Pierre stood farther away again, slouching against the wall, watching her curiously.

"Scooby-Doo socks, hm?"

At first his question didn't really register, then she flashed her eyes down toward her socks. Yes, she'd forgotten, but she'd pulled on her knee-high Scooby socks that morning.

"They were a gift," she said haughtily, honesty prompting her to add, "but I do love Scooby-Doo. And they *were* covered by my boots…although I don't know why I'm explaining anything to you," she finished huffily, annoyed that she'd bothered. She didn't like Pierre. He was an overbearing brute who'd insulted her and made her feel about two feet tall at the party where she'd met him. She just had to keep reminding herself.

He shrugged in a way that said that he wasn't bothered by her attitude. Or that was what she thought the shrug meant.

"Would you like to come sit by the fire while we talk? I was just about to fix a hot toddy, if you're interested. My own twist, with some good Canadian maple liqueur thrown in."

Marina found herself oddly reluctant to get any closer to Pierre, but her logic kicked in again as well. She was, in all likelihood, truly trapped with him. There wasn't anything else to do except go lock herself in a bedroom and sit on the bed, probably brooding. More, her feet were starting to feel cold on the hard floor.

"That *does* sound nice. I think my toes need to thaw out a little," she admitted.

Pierre smiled, making his eyes crinkle at the corners. The crinkles told her that he must smile a lot, which seemed a bit incongruous with everything she knew and had heard about him.

"The Great Room is just through here." He gestured toward the doorway where he'd come from, waiting for her to step through it first before he followed. She stopped abruptly, and he nearly ran into her, but she couldn't help but stare at how large and cozy the room was. Two or more stories tall, with log-lined balconies, the Great Room was a study in contrasts between stylish modern touches and classic Vermont cabin. What had made her stop short, though, was the incredible workmanship of the mantel, which was much taller than she was, filled with a blazing fire, and flanked by two marble sculptures of growling wolves.

"Exquisite," she breathed, temporarily forgetting her companion in her enthusiasm. She walked toward the wolves, running her hand along the sharp teeth and fur on the head of one of them. Whoever had carved these must have been a true master. Of course, she thought wryly, the Gaspards only bought the best.

"You like our *loups-garous*?" The question was casual, but there was something behind Pierre's words. Something more.

"I love them," she admitted. "Stunning craftsmanship. They could be in a museum." She paused. "Isn't a *loup-garou* a werewolf?"

Pierre nodded. "Aha, you remember more of your high-school French than Annelise does, I think."

Again, Marina smiled in spite of herself. "I studied harder," she said. "I wanted to be ready to travel…well, wherever we were sent." The words were out of her mouth before she could think or decide against mentioning the past. She waited for the familiar regret, the sadness at the recognition that the life she'd dreamed of having with Jaime was never going to happen, and he was still gone forever. The sadness came, but it was muted. She focused on the werewolves again.

"Interesting choice of subject for the sculptor…but inspired." She studied the eyes. Somehow, the cold, smooth stone had been transformed into something living and breathing. The eyes looked incredibly lifelike, both savage and proud, but most of all, aware…like a humans.

"Contradictions are so interesting, don't you think?" Pierre's comment sounded offhand, but the expression on his face was intense. Then he smiled again, a charming, bright smile that she imagined must serve him well at public events, and the odd intensity was gone. "Here I am talking when you should be warming your toes and I should be making us those drinks, eh?"

Why did it have to be her? Pierre asked himself. But of course, he thought ruefully, the universe would never miss such a good opportunity to keep him humble. He'd been acting to protect his family when he'd spoken so harshly to her at that party at the Mount Valder, but he also knew he'd been an ass to her. He could have gotten his point across more gently, but instead, he'd been the harsh dictator his critics so often accused him of being. The ruthless businessman, head of a company that had quarterly profits larger than the GDP of many countries. The quaver in her voice, coupled with the fierce rigidity of her spine as she'd left that darkened conference room, had haunted his dreams since that night. He'd actually been starting to like her so, like the bastard that he was — that he'd *had* to be his entire adult life — he'd put her in her place. Viciously.

He'd hoped to stay distant from her, only interacting politely as needed at events with Rémy. But now…distance was going to be impossible. *Merde alors.* He let himself be comforted by the familiar feel of preparing the drinks in the kitchen. The feeling of home and comfort was stronger here for him than in any of their other houses, which was why he'd decided on the spur of the moment to come up early for Rémy and Annelise's engagement party. Obviously, he should have checked first. Normally, he would have. He'd been so edgy lately, though. Paranoid. Seeing possible attackers around every corner.

Guess one nearly successful attempted murder by poisoning will do that to a man, he thought dryly. His entire body still ached from the experience, but his throat most of all. He knew his voice would never be the same, in spite of all the expensive medical care he'd received. And for what? The twisted agenda and revenge of a man he'd once called a friend?

He was fighting to make peace with the rage he felt about how close Claude had come to killing his sister. *And you*, the same small voice reminded him. Claude had come very close to killing Pierre. Suddenly, after the attack, all his intense focus on appearances and luxury, on carrying on the proud family tradition, had melted into nothingness. The only things left behind were his love for and devotion to his family. Well, and a laser focus on their safety. He had always favored this small cabin in Vermont—relatively small, of course, since he knew that it was a very good size—but now that he was so concerned with safety, he loved its remote location and general inaccessibility even more.

He stirred the two mugs, absently noting that he'd finished making their drinks without conscious thought. Then again, this kitchen was deeply familiar to him, filled with happy memories of past hiking trips with his parents. His siblings were probably too young to remember, but Pierre had been old enough to recall the time long before his mother had grown so ill, when they would come to this cabin for weekend retreats. *'To smell the pines,'* his mother had said. Pierre was the one who had steered Rémy toward using the cabin and the lodge nearby, which they also owned, for the small engagement party. He had only himself to blame for his uncomfortable predicament now. It would just be a hell of lot easier if he didn't suspect that he was starting to like Marina more than he should. He couldn't help a small smile as he recalled how adorable her feet had looked in those ridiculous socks.

Chapter Three

With her feet warming nicely in front of the blazing fire and her hands cupped around the heated mug full of the aromatic maple hot toddy that Pierre had brought to her, Marina was starting to feel much better. Of course, part of that might have been the two long sips she'd taken of the extremely alcoholic drink on top of an empty stomach from skipping lunch to get on the road earlier. Whatever the reason, she was on her way to feeling good, in spite of the circumstances.

Until she looked over at Pierre and scowled. He glanced over at her expression, but instead of looking offended, his eyes flashed with amusement and he looked like his lips might be curving into a smile.

"What is your American saying? Should we talk about the hippopotamus in the room?"

A snort of laughter escaped Marina's nose before she could stop it. "Um, I think you mean 'elephant' in the room."

Pierre waved his hand dismissively in a distinctly French gesture. "Hippopotamus, elephant, rhinoceros — they are all very similar. It makes the same sense."

"Elephants are bigger," she argued, wondering why it even mattered. Pierre just made her want to be contrary. *Except when you first met him,* the little voice in her head reminded her. *Then, you didn't want to be contrary at all.*

Pierre's eyes crinkled at the corners. "I concede, *chérie.* Now can we talk about the pachyderm?"

"Maybe you should clarify what you mean," Marina hedged.

Pierre sighed. "You know I'm referring to our… conversation the night we met."

Marina shifted on the couch cushions which had felt so welcoming just a moment earlier. "You're direct, huh? Like to go right for the throat?"

Pierre nodded gravely. "I've been told that before, quite often by business competitors." He paused and looked…uncomfortable? She wasn't certain, and his expression went carefully blank again before she could be sure. "I think it may be that this attitude doesn't serve me as well in my personal life, though."

"You think?" she answered, raising her eyebrow meaningfully. He had had a point, though. "Much as I dislike the way you spoke to me and made me feel, you weren't wrong. When I apologized, I meant it, and I have been, and will continue to be, much more careful. I think it mortified me most to not only behave so badly but also to have someone call me out on it." She had always prided herself on being honest and direct, too, even when another attitude would have served her better.

She could tell from his raised eyebrows that she'd surprised him.

"I was unnecessarily cruel," he answered, surprising her in turn. Her shock must have been written on her face. "Does it stun you so much that I admit I was wrong?" Beneath his casual veneer, she could feel that he was waiting on her answer.

"Yes," she answered baldly. "I mean, from everything I have ever heard about you, you aren't a man who likely even admits to himself when he has miscalculated."

His dark eyes were fathomless as the reflection of the flames flickered in them for an instant. "Pierre Gaspard, CEO of Gaspard Industries and head of the Gaspard family...that man cannot afford to show any weakness like regret."

"Who are you, if not Pierre Gaspard?" she countered.

"Who indeed?" he answered, then leaned forward with an oddly intent expression. "Whoever I am, though, I do regret hurting your feelings. I was harsher than I needed to be to get you to understand the world that your best friend has now entered—that *you* have entered as well, by association."

She sighed, trying to hold on to her anger at him but feeling it slip away like a wisp of silk. "I should have known better. I don't... It isn't like me to open up to a stranger in any way. It's just that I felt an odd connection to you in that room—" She broke off when she realized how much she was saying. "What *were* you doing there, anyway?" She blurted out the first question she could think of—anything to change the subject a bit.

"Again, *chérie*, I'll tell you mine if you tell me yours." The self-assurance in his eyes told her that he knew she didn't want to tell him. *Damn it, he's right.*

"Let's just call a temporary truce, instead?" She made the statement a question and hated the little quaver in her voice.

He held out his hand, his smile slightly mocking. "But of course."

When she reached for his hand, he surprised her. Instead of shaking hers, he held it to his lips. The heat of his soft kiss on the back of her hand stunned her and made her snatch hers back as though he'd burned it.

"Why did you do that?" she demanded, but the effect was ruined by how breathless her voice was.

He shrugged as if it meant nothing. "To seal our truce, of course." His laugh was dark and rich. "You Americans and your prudish ways. You never kiss?"

She narrowed her eyes. "Not usually, no. That's... I mean, nobody does that kind of hand-kiss thing outside the movies," she huffed.

"A pity," he drawled.

She continued to eye him suspiciously. The silence hung heavy between them, so quiet that she jumped when one of the logs snapped in the fire.

"Poor *Marinette*. Don't worry. You're not stranded with the big, bad wolf, you know."

She pounced on the change of subject.

"Are we really sure that there's no way to leave? I mean, you can't want to be stuck here with me any more than I want to be stuck with you. And bummer for Annelise and Rémy... We'll have to postpone their party for sure." Even to her own ears, her arguments sounded weak.

"I'm glad you have so much faith in my family's wealth and power to buy us everything, *chérie*, but I'm afraid that even if I had our helicopter here, we wouldn't be able to fly it. At the very least, we're stuck until the snow stops, and that could be quite a while if the reports on the radio are to be believed." He paused, considering. "We could probably make it to the main lodge the day after tomorrow, either on a snowmobile or snowshoes, but no farther than that. It's pretty remote out here."

Marina frowned, but she remembered how long it had taken her to get there from the main road. "Do you think everyone will know not to try to come to the party?"

His nod was brief. "*Absolument*. Yes. I'm certain Marc and Villiers, our family's head of security, are following the weather conditions and will have realized the storm was much worse than predicted."

She was relieved that no one else would get stuck out in the storm, and she allowed herself to sink a little more into the cushions, until another concern popped into her head. "Do we have enough supplies to get through this?"

Pierre's chuckle was indulgent. "No worries on that front. The caretakers always keep this place stocked enough to host an army. They tease that it's because I eat like an army—" He stopped abruptly, a pained expression flashing on his face.

"Do you come here very often?" she asked.

He looked away for a moment and she thought he wouldn't answer, but he surprised her. "More often than anyone except George and Bonnie are aware. Especially since my accident."

She put her hand out to touch his knee and she felt almost an electric shock of heat on her palm where they touched. Pierre tensed, but he didn't move away.

"You *were* injured. I *knew* it." Honesty compelled her to continue. "Or, actually, you know what I thought at first, but after we met, I knew that the reason you stayed out of the limelight and away from the business for so long must have been something else. Something more serious. What happened?"

At that last question, he stiffened again, and his expression closed. "Nothing that I want to talk about." His tone was clipped and forbidding. He cleared his throat. "Anyway, at least you understand we have more than enough food—"

"*Oh Dios!*" Marina groaned.

His expression transformed to instant concern, and he looked her over from head to toe. "You're hurt. I knew I should have demanded to check you over when you arrived."

Marina raised her eyebrows. "Um, nope. You do not get to *demand* anything—even if we have a truce, I'm not one of your underlings."

"One of my…*underlings*, as you so charmingly call them, would have sense enough to tell me if he or she was hurt. I may be demanding in all ways, but I take care of my own."

Marina wanted to continue to glare at him, but his words held a dark appeal. She was used to being on her own, to always taking care of herself and others, but she'd secretly longed to be taken care of and cherished again. Pierre was obviously a control freak, but…was it really so wrong to cede to him a little more?

She took a deep breath and shook her head. "I'm not really hurt—not badly anyway, although my neck is starting to feel pretty stiff. I just realized I forgot that I have four dozen cupcakes from the fanciest bakery on Newbury Street in the trunk of the SUV. They're probably little cupcake-cicles by now. All the little mini-engagement ring decorations on the tops are probably broken, too."

"Did you park in the garage?" he asked, looking toward one side of the room. "I didn't hear the garage door, but the storm is pretty loud."

Marina's heart sank and she groaned again. "No...I couldn't get all the way up the road. There was a huge tree down and the SUV just slid into it." She looked up at him apologetically. "I'm so sorry, but I think it might be totaled. It was Rémy's...or maybe it was your family's? God, I feel so bad for wrecking it. I'll pay for any repairs."

Pierre shook his head emphatically, making one dark curl fall onto his forehead, softening his expression. "*Non, non*, please. Don't worry about the vehicle. I'm just glad you weren't hurt badly in the crash. Objects are just things. People can never be replaced."

Marina studied his face. "I think you really mean that," she said.

Pierre narrowed his eyes and looked genuinely affronted. "Of course I do. What kind of a monster thinks that a vehicle is more important than a young woman's health and safety?"

Something warm flickered to life inside her at those words, but the warmth turned to a shiver as she imagined what would have happened if she hadn't taken Annelise and Rémy up on their offer to loan her their SUV.

"What is it, *chérie*?" Pierre asked. She should have been surprised he could sense her mood so easily, but she wasn't. Not anymore. She was coming to understand that Pierre Gaspard was someone who was a master at reading people and situations.

She looked at the fire as she answered. "I just realized that if I'd driven my hatchback here instead of the SUV, I might have been injured pretty badly." She tried to shrug, but it was a sobering thought. "I guess I'm lucky to have such a bossy best friend."

"You are very lucky." Pierre's eyes were envious for a second — she was certain she didn't imagine that — but when he looked at her again, it was with deep concern, underlaid with obvious self-reproach. "You should have told me immediately that you'd been in an accident, *chérie*. I insist on examining you."

His words weren't sexual, but something about the way his voice deepened and went gravelly at the end made her pulse quicken and her breath speed up. He sounded implacable, as if he would hold her down with his large, strong-looking hands if she dared to refuse. *For Heaven's sake*, she chided herself, *he asked to examine you, not tear off your clothes.*

"Do you... Are you trained in first-aid or something?"

Pierre's laugh was bitter. "Or something. We had so many attempted kidnappings when we were children that our parents insisted that we take a wide range of classes on... Let's just call them *unorthodox* subjects. Many different styles of fighting, which Rémy and Luc loved, defensive driving, wilderness survival and basic wilderness medicine. Papa was a paranoid bastard, but we've all had to use our skills more than once."

"Wow," Marina answered, stunned at the stark picture that Pierre's words painted of their childhood. "Attempted kidnappings?"

He nodded slowly. "Mostly amateur attempts, a few really professional. We had a young nanny we all liked who sold information about us to some very bad people. I think that one was the worst. Well, until last year."

"What happened to the nanny?" she asked.

His expression grew grim. "Papa wanted her prosecuted, but we argued—*I* argued—that we should be merciful since the plans hadn't succeeded. The police let her go, but we found out that she was murdered the next day, probably by whoever she'd been working with. She had a sick mother in the United States whose insurance wouldn't cover the treatment she needed. That was what we discovered after she died. I would have given her the money myself, just from my allowance."

Marina's heart went out to the young Pierre. *How absolutely horrible to live with something like that. How will he ever trust anyone?*

"Pierre, I'm—"

He cut her off brusquely. "So, you see I'm more than qualified to act as your physician, at least for tonight. If you agree?" His words were businesslike, but something in his eyes forbade her from mentioning the personal story again.

"Please," Marina agreed, holding his gaze.

"Where are you feeling pain? And how severe is it?"

Marina closed her eyes for a moment, taking stock of her body. When she opened them again, Pierre's gaze was intent. It was as if she'd caught an unguarded glimpse behind the mask. She felt another warm flare of attraction that was totally inappropriate in the circumstances.

"My neck is stiff, and I have a headache. I definitely hit the tree trunk pretty hard and I remember my neck and head slammed back on the seat. And I think I must have scraped my arm scrambling over the log, and maybe turned my knee a bit. I wasn't really paying attention at the time—just trying to get here in one piece. None of it feels horrible, though."

Pierre set down his drink and took hers from her hand with a warm brush of hard fingertips, leaving both cups on the coffee table. He moved closer so that she could smell his fresh, woodsy scent, spicy and delicious. He stared at her eyes for a moment.

"Your pupils appear normal," he observed. "Your eyes are stunning. Such an unusual color, especially with your dark hair," he added almost absently, and she felt heat rise in her cheeks at the offhanded compliment.

"Thanks," she breathed. "My mother's family was Irish, and my father was half-Cuban, half-Welsh, so I got dark hair and skin with true aquamarine eyes. My nana — my brother and I were basically raised by her, our father's mother — says that she knew I was meant to be named Marina even before my eyes became this color. She thinks she has a touch of 'the Sight'." Marina shut her mouth with a snap. She couldn't believe how much she'd been rambling. Sure, she'd had about half of a strong drink, but she wasn't usually spilling her guts to anyone this quickly. *Or ever*, she mentally amended. Especially not someone she didn't even like, although she wasn't as sure now that what she felt for Pierre was intense dislike. Still, even if she didn't actively dislike him, he wasn't going to ever be her best friend, for Heaven's sake.

"They really *are* the color of the ocean, aren't they? But the Caribbean, not the rocky, cold North Atlantic we have up here." He cut off his own musings abruptly, clearing his throat again. It seemed to be something he did often.

"Can you move your head all around on your neck?" His tone was businesslike and clinical. "Do it very gently, though. Don't move it if you start to feel any real pain. We don't want you to do any more damage," he cautioned, watching her movements carefully as she rolled her head very slowly around. Tipping it forward stretched the stiffness, but nothing made her gasp.

"It's tender," she admitted, "especially when I move it forward, but it's not horrible. More achy than anything."

He flattened his lips with displeasure and a little line appeared between his dark eyebrows. He seemed angry, but she sensed it wasn't directed at her. "We'll have to see how you feel tomorrow to be sure, but that's a good sign, at least." He looked down at her legs. "I'm going to roll up your trousers now."

"My *trousers*?" Marina couldn't help her laughter.

Pierre's dark eyes were thunderous, his annoyance obvious. "Isn't that the word? I'm afraid I don't have many non-business conversations in English."

"Well, it's a perfectly fine word if you're a proper Victorian gentleman, and I know that other English-speaking countries use it more often, but...no. I just can't let you call my leggings trousers, certainly not when you're talking about taking them off! I'm an American and I'm wearing pants."

His expression grew rugged, subtly more dangerous, and there was a flare of unmistakable desire flickering behind his chocolate-brown eyes. "*Pants*, are they? We were taught by our British tutor that that was a word we weren't supposed to use."

Marina's pulse quickened again. "What does it mean in England?"

"What do you call your undergarment — the one that is currently hugging your sexy little ass? Panties?"

Marina nodded, thinking that it was ridiculous how hearing those words in his rasping, sensual voice made her insides quiver.

He raised his eyebrows meaningfully, and she understood.

She burst out laughing, which seemed to surprise him, but a slow smile lit his face and eyes, making him look almost boyish.

"Is it that funny, *chérie*?" he asked, raising one eyebrow.

"No," she gasped. "Only I just realized how suggestive Eduardo's British friend was being when he said he fancied the pants off Annelise."

Instantly, Pierre's expression hardened. "Who is Eduardo? One of your lovers?"

"Um, whoa there, killer. Eduardo is my brother." She waved her hands as if to ward him off. "Not that it's any of your business," she added.

"Who is his friend? Rémy will not be pleased to hear another man has been expressing a strong interest in Annelise."

Marina thought that was probably putting it mildly. Rémy was crazy in love with Annelise, and anyone who tried to hit on her would probably have to have a death wish. "Oh my God, *relax*. His name is Rupert, he's RAF and he and my brother met on some peacekeeping mission. He hit on Annelise last year, right after she broke up with Kyle, that ratfink." She paused. "Kyle is the ratfink, Rupert is perfectly nice," she clarified. "Well, even though he's a nice guy, Annelise wasn't interested and turned him down. She was so miserable I'm not even sure she realized she was turning him down — then she met your brother and that was that."

"If he's a nice guy, are *you* interested in or involved with this Rupert?" Pierre's voice sounded dangerous, low and rumbly.

"Again, none of your business, but no. I don't... I never...just no." She couldn't believe what she'd almost said, and a hot blush rose back into her cheeks.

Pierre studied her face, seeming to judge her sincerity. She thought he'd press for more information, but he dropped it.

"So, now that we've established that Rupert is a nice man who nobody is interested in, poor fellow, will you shift your legs so I can I roll up your *pants*?" The way he said it, putting a subtle emphasis on 'pants', made something deep inside her stretch with excitement. If she wasn't careful, she was afraid that Nice Pierre, as opposed to Brooding Pierre, might just be able to charm the panties off of her. She grimaced as she straightened her legs to give him easier access, and he knelt down in front of her.

"Go ahead," she answered, her voice a little more than a whisper. She gestured at her leg. "It's my right knee."

His hands were firm and capable, but surprisingly tender as he rolled up one leg of her legging. Her knee was already beginning to swell, and it was red with darker patches of what would likely become bruises.

"That looks pretty rough," Pierre winced sympathetically when he had it uncovered. "That must hurt, *chérie*. I'm surprised it didn't bother you as you were walking here."

She bit her bottom lip. "Honestly? I was too cold to notice anything else. It didn't really start hurting at all until we were sitting by the fire, warming up."

He nodded. "That makes sense." He ran his hands over it with aching gentleness, but she still sucked in a sharp breath at the pain from his touch. "It's going to be an ugly bruise and probably going to swell more. Can you move it at all?"

Marina gingerly moved her leg. "It hurts like hell, but yeah."

Pierre studied her face. "It's good that you can move it—probably twisted or sprained as opposed to broken—but I am so sorry you were hurt."

"It's not your fault," Marina answered.

"Even so," he countered, "I would never wish to see you in pain." His eyes blazed for an instant. He coughed as if to cover the emotion, and nearly leapt to his feet. "I'll go get an ice pack for your knee, and the first-aid kit for your arm."

She smiled in spite of herself at the fanciful notion that she'd driven the notoriously cold and powerful Pierre Gaspard into the kitchen. He was turning out not to be what she'd thought he was. Not at all.

Chapter Four

Pain. The pain was assaulting Marina from all sides in the weak morning light, followed by confusion as she glanced around the spacious room. The previous day's events came rushing back to her and she rolled onto her stomach, pressing her face into her pillow with a groan. Pierre had insisted on taking care of her injuries, then he'd made them a snack, which she'd devoured so quickly that he was probably counting himself lucky that she hadn't nipped the hand he'd carried the tray with. Once she'd been full of food and HAD finished her maple hot toddy, as well as the pain pills he'd insisted she take for the swelling, she had just made it upstairs to one of the guest bedrooms to flop down onto the bed, too tired to even think of finding PJs.

Well, she didn't care what he thought of her manners. They were stranded together, and until less than twelve hours ago, she had intended to try to avoid him as much as possible for the foreseeable future. It wasn't as if they were on vacation together, for God's sake.

She turned her face to the side so she could breathe better, and the movement made her head and neck throb. She needed more pain pills, for sure. Her new position allowed her to smell the faint but delicious scent of bacon cooking, and her stomach gave a pitiful gurgle. *Correction*, she thought, *I need pain pills and bacon*.

The ache in her knee was sharp as she staggered to her feet. She'd always heard that the day after a car accident was usually much worse than the day of, and she could now attest to that. Every part of her felt as though it had been hammered with a mallet, and she feared that more than half of her body was one big bruise. She was suddenly glad Pierre had insisted on treating her fully, even though she'd never tell him that.

She staggered over to the door and cracked it open but realized as she hung on to the doorjamb that she hadn't even bothered to dig through her purse, the only luggage she'd brought in, to try to find a hairbrush.

"I'm glad you're up, *chérie*. I was just starting to worry." The sound of Pierre's voice breaking into the muffled morning silence made pulse rate spike and her heart felt like it climbed right up into her throat. The inside of the cabin was dark, and she didn't see him anywhere nearby.

"I think my body wishes I wasn't awake," she answered, trying for a light tone but failing miserably.

"I drew you a bath." His words grew louder as if he were getting closer, although she still couldn't see him. He sounded as dark and raspy in the morning as he had the night before, and there was an answering shiver deep within her. "I put some clean clothes in the bathroom for you. My sister left some things here last time we came, and I think they'll fit you. I would have come in while you were sleeping, but I thought you might object."

His silhouette rose into view, tall and dark, as he reached the top of the stairs, and he stepped into a dim ray of light so that she could see him. The reason that he was so silent became apparent when she spotted the cozy-looking leather slippers he wore.

"You're damn right I would have objected," she huffed.

He raised one eyebrow, looking amused. "Now I feel as though I might have missed something worth seeing. Still, I suppose it's better that I didn't give in to my baser impulses to find out what you wear to sleep."

She almost argued again but instead forced herself to relax. "Thank you," she said sarcastically. "Wait! Did you say you drew a bath?"

He nodded, his eyes intent on her face.

"I, uh, that's really thoughtful of you." She didn't know why she was feeling so awkward with him.

"I'm the eldest of four children, after all. I did take care of my younger siblings, especially Clothilde. Is it so hard to believe I can fill a tub with water and bath salts for my injured guest?" He stepped closer and she could smell the wool of his sweater, mixed with his sexy, spicy scent that made her nose twitch with appreciation. She didn't realize she was just standing there, sniffing him, until he spoke again.

"Do you need help, *Marinette*?" His eyes gleamed, and he brushed the column of her neck with one rough fingertip. Her nipples tightened and goosebumps rose on her neck and chest. "I could carry you there, help you undress…"

Marina rocked back, and the small movement caused another spasm of hurt in her knee, neck and head. It broke whatever strange spell Pierre's words had woven, and he pulled his hand away.

"I'll be fine," she answered, her words a little too quick.

Pierre pursed his lips and stepped back to give her some space. Not much space, though, she noted. She would have to practically brush against him to get by.

"Now that *is* a pity," he murmured. He turned away and headed back toward the stairs. "Breakfast will still be warm when you finish, so just come on into the kitchen whenever."

"Great," she mumbled, trying to be nice but concentrating too hard on moving her sore body down the hallway to be anything but surly.

"Oh, and Marina?"

She paused and turned to half-look back over her shoulder at him.

"If you change your mind or find you can't scrub your back, just shout. I'll hear you, and I'll come to you."

What the hell are you doing? Pierre asked himself as he padded back down the stairs to the kitchen. Even as he tried to stop the action, he found he was straining his ears for a hint of a sound, a warning that Marina might need him. *Merde alors*, even if she weren't his future sister-in-law's best friend and thus off-limits, she wasn't for him. He knew what he needed in a woman, and it was so rare that he'd stopped looking a long time ago.

Still…what could it hurt to indulge himself a little? It had been so long since he'd felt a hint of genuine interest, both in himself and from a woman in a warm, willing body, that he reveled in the novelty. Oh, women were all over him almost everywhere he went. He knew he was good-looking, appealing to women, even without his fortune and power. With it, though, he was nigh on irresistible.

When he'd been younger, he'd been conflicted. He'd loved the attention, but he'd felt like it had just come too easily. Now that he was older and jaded—in so many ways—he just longed for one woman, just *one*, to see beyond the package of his handsome exterior and money and power to the man who he assiduously kept hidden. It was unfair, of course, since he never let anyone see beyond the façade. Well, anyone except his family, of course. He pushed women away then blamed them for it. But Marina had caught him off-guard twice—first at the family party, then again here in his refuge.

That must be it, he reasoned. He just liked that she had seen a little of the real Pierre. Well, and she was fucking gorgeous. *Putain*, she was tall and elegant, slim but with generous curves where it counted. His cock had gone rock-hard just thinking about her pert, curvy ass the night before. He'd had to adjust himself when he'd touched her leg as he examined her injuries. *Her leg*, for God's sake. It wasn't even an erotic zone.

The rich scent of freshly-ground coffee beans rose around his face, sharpening all of his senses, as he poured the thick powder into the espresso machine. Again, the familiar motions of making food and drinks in the kitchen soothed him, and he let his thoughts drift back to Marina. He could picture her upstairs in the bathroom, naked in the enormous tub, water sluicing off her soft skin—the soft skin that he'd touched twice now. His fingers practically itched to touch her again and to find out how soft she was everywhere else. *Merde encore*, there he went again with the inappropriate thoughts.

Rémy would flay him alive if his brother knew how Pierre had treated Annelise's best friend at the party. His brother adored his fiancée, was completely crazy about her and wouldn't stand to have so much as a hair on her head touched. Marina was obviously more than a friend to Annelise, more like a sister. Frankly, Pierre was shocked that Marina hadn't said anything to Annelise about how he'd spoken to her at the Mount Valder—and she definitely hadn't, because he knew Rémy would have called or come to find him at once and probably slammed his fist into his chin.

Still, Pierre's mild deception, then basically kicking Marina out of the party, paled in comparison to what he was contemplating now. If he listened to his body, he would lay Marina out in every room of the cabin and fuck her until she couldn't walk—until she wouldn't *want* to walk. He would bring her pleasure like she'd never known, and she would be damned passionate in return. He could tell that there was a well of untapped fire inside her, waiting, banked, for the right man to stoke the flames. He could most definitely be that man. His hands twitched on the hot coffee mugs as he imagined what it would feel like to have her go wild in his arms, to lap her juices from the source, to sink into her molten, velvet depths.

Merde, he couldn't remember how long it had been since he'd made love to a woman. He'd had mindless sex with someone he'd met at a party about six months earlier, and he'd made certain that she'd had a good time, but it had been much, much longer since he'd really cared for his partner. He had the uncomfortable realization that maybe he'd never really *cared* about any of his lovers. The kind of man who that showed him to be wasn't the kind of man who should be thinking of touching a woman he would have to see regularly at family events for the rest of his life. Marina might be naïve and impulsive, but she certainly didn't deserve to be ravished and abandoned by a soulless asshole like him.

A long time ago, he had been young and carefree. Well, perhaps 'carefree' was the wrong word, since he'd always had to look after his younger siblings and cover for his parents' benign neglect—but he hadn't always had the burden of being the head of the family, the CEO, President and Chairman of the Board of Directors of Gaspard Industries—and a popular minor celebrity, in spite of his efforts to avoid the limelight. At some point between giving up on any dreams he'd held for himself alone after his parents had died and finding pictures in magazines of himself with nearly any woman he had genuinely tried to connect with when he'd been barely out of his teens, he'd become harder. Colder. Weary of tricks and suspicious of almost everyone, he'd started to care only for his family. When he took lovers, he wanted them to know the score, too. There would be no sweet kisses, no cuddling in the morning light and certainly no ten-carat diamond and champagne at the end of any dinners.

He'd grown even more paranoid after the attempt on Clothilde's life almost a year before, searching for conspiracies and jumping at shadows. Then, after he'd been attacked and nearly poisoned to death several months earlier, what little faith he might have had left in humanity in general had been snuffed out entirely.

He had mostly retreated from everything and everyone, at first because he had been physically recovering, then because he didn't want to be around anyone who wasn't his brothers or sister. He'd even had dark suspicions about his brother's fiancée, although he had to admit now how happy she made Rémy. When had every day become so much the same, though? He couldn't pinpoint the date, but he knew that for a while now, he'd felt like he was only going through the motions of living. Acting so cruelly to Marina at the party had woken him up to what he'd started to become.

He liked control. Of course, he *had* to stay focused and collected, in control of his emotions at all times under ridiculous pressure as the head of one of the largest companies in the world, but he craved it in every area. He didn't just want to dominate his lovers. He *needed* to. Therein was the problem.

He didn't want a woman to just *act* like he owned her because she was playing, although he certainly didn't judge anyone else for indulging in any games they wished. No, he wanted a woman to *know* he owned her, that she belonged to him utterly. Completely. Every breath she drew would be for him, her first thought when she woke would be of him and she would fall asleep with his cock buried deep inside her. But he didn't let anyone close enough to truly feel that way, because if she belonged to him, wouldn't she then have to hold at least a part of him? He never wanted anyone to have that sort of power over him again, not after his crappy childhood. If he were going to give up everything, he could damn well live as he chose, on his own terms only, and everyone else could just fuck off.

No matter how gorgeous and sexy and refreshing he found Marina to be — and *putain*, she was certainly all of those things — and no matter whether he thought she might actually be able to give him the things he needed, she was not for him. Or rather, *he* was not for *her*. He sensed that they could be amazing together — fucking spectacular. They would light each other's bodies on fire. Then he would leave her, because that was what he did. He would almost certainly break her heart, and he might ruin his relationship with his own brother, because Rémy would try to kill him.

Pierre should have heard Marina coming, but he'd been so lost in his thoughts that the rustling sound close behind him made him jump and spin around instinctively. She gasped, raw fear flashing across her face at his murderous expression, and he loathed himself for making her afraid, even for an instant. He was always careful around his family to not let them see how cold and angry he had become — and how lethal — but she'd surprised him into revealing his unschooled expression. He deliberately relaxed his muscles and tried for a smile but he thought maybe it was more of a grimace.

"So sorry… You startled me. Did the bath help?" His words were gruff, and he cleared his throat. Something about the poison that had nearly killed him had done permanent damage to his throat, lungs and vocal cords. It was still painful if he spoke too much or let his throat get really dry, although it was a damn sight better than it had been.

"So much," she answered. "Thank you. The bath salts were awesome, too." She stretched her arms wide and wiggled her fingers, making the borrowed shirt pull across her chest tightly in an unconsciously seductive way he was certain she wasn't aware of. "I feel almost like myself. Well, like a B-movie horror version of myself, but I'll take it."

She shifted her weight from one foot to the other and he noted that she was just enough curvier than his lithe sister that the clothes hugged her like a second skin around her breasts and hips. It was cozy in the kitchen, but even the thick cabin walls couldn't keep out every single draft, and her nipples beaded to visible points under her sweater, which couldn't completely hide them.

"You didn't like *all* of the clothes?" he asked, his voice gone husky as he couldn't tear his eyes off the generous mounds of her breasts, which were clearly not covered by the bra he had left for her.

Her cheeks flushed pink and he longed to feel how hot they were.

"Thank you… It was really thoughtful of you to lay out some clothes for me. I must be, um, a bit bigger than your sister, because the bra was tight and it was too hard on my muscles to wrestle it on. I didn't think you would really be able to tell."

God, she was priceless. Any red-blooded man would give a great deal of money to see Marina braless, and she had no idea.

"*Chérie*, I would have to be either blind or on my deathbed not to notice your spectacular breasts. In fact, even if I were dying, I think I'd still try to trick you into brushing them against my chest to give me one last sweet memory to take to the afterlife."

Her expression was a mix of horror and fascination, all underlaid with unwilling interest. He quirked his lips up in a wry smile.

"But you never have to feel anything close to bad about that. Any man should be humbled and grateful any time you don't wear a bra."

Her cheeks took on the rosy glow that he thought he would never get enough of seeing and she pursed her lips. "I, uh, thank you?" she answered at last, making something in his chest loosen.

Bon Dieu, he wished the bra had fit. Keeping his distance was going to be a constant struggle.

* * * *

Marina didn't know what to make of Pierre's comments — or his attitude. He was such an odd combination, harsh and brooding one minute but preparing her a bath and cooking her a surprisingly delicious breakfast the next. Following his suggestive comments about her breasts, he'd served breakfast for the two of them at the cozy, round table in the kitchen. The warmth of the strong coffee, along with the mouth-watering food, which she'd devoured like a starving person, were making her feel lazy and content as she pushed her plate back and stretched out her legs. They had eaten mostly in silence, almost by mutual consent, but it hadn't been uncomfortable.

"Any more news on the storm?" she asked tentatively, looking again outside at the swirling mass of thick snowflakes and howling wind that made it look like the cabin was completely blanketed by the blizzard.

A little line appeared between Pierre's dark eyebrows as he frowned. "Nothing good. It's potentially even more severe than predicted. They said something about the collision between high- and low-pressure fronts on either side, so it could be stuck on top of us for a couple of days now."

Marina sighed. "Poor Annelise! She was so excited for this party. I just hope she's not worried."

Pierre's dark eyes were inscrutable as he studied her face with an intensity that was uncomfortable. "The cell phone reception is almost non-existent, and the landlines and Internet are down, but I managed to get a message out on my sat phone, so everyone will know we're all right. If we didn't have a generator, though, we would surely have lost power last night."

Although it wasn't good news, his words lifted a weight off of her that she hadn't realized had been so heavy. She'd hated picturing Annelise, or her brother and her nana, worrying away that she might have slid off into some snowy ditch on the side of a deserted Vermont highway. Annelise would have been feeling guilty, even though no one was to blame for the weather being way worse than predicted.

"Thank you," she said — and meant it whole-heartedly.

"I tell you we're stuck for a few more days, with no communications, no transportation and only a generator, and you thank me like you really mean it. I can hardly believe it, *chérie*."

Marina shifted on the cushioned kitchen chair. "I'm not jumping for joy — not that I could jump far right now anyway." She laughed dryly. "But as long as we're not going to freeze or starve and everyone knows we're safe, I can deal."

Pierre studied her again until she began to feel like a particularly puzzling specimen under a microscope.

"What?" she asked when she couldn't stand it anymore.

He shrugged. "I guess the women I'm used to are difficult."

She laughed. She could imagine what kind of women he was used to. She'd seen the perfect beauties that always seemed to surround him in every picture printed by the Canadian and French press. They wore designer gowns, had artfully messy highlighted hair, and probably got mani-pedis every week. If she hadn't gotten her nails done with Annelise, she could have gone months without visiting a salon, and she kept her hair long and natural. She'd never owned a designer gown and fully expected that the closest she would continue to get to them would be drooling over the window displays on Newbury Street. Still, it wasn't as though she wasn't difficult sometimes.

"Thanks, I think, but I have my moments." Then she thought about what he had said. "Hold up. Are you calling me easy?" she teased.

His rich chuckle rolled through the room and seemed to fill every corner with warmth. It was a genuine sound, surprised and happy. "I wouldn't dare!" He held up his hands as if to ward off an attack, then grabbed their two plates.

She was so shocked that he would do the dishes, on top of having cooked, that she almost missed the words he muttered under his breath.

"A man can dream, though, can't he?"

Chapter Five

In spite of all the energy she'd thought she had right after breakfast, she was still tired from her injuries. At Pierre's insistence, she'd gratefully gone back to bed to rest under the fluffy duvet. When she woke up again, the light was dim, but with the storm, that meant it could be any time of day. She felt a surge of excitement that she couldn't immediately identify the cause of, then almost groaned when she realized it was because she was looking forward to seeing *him* again. *Pierre Gaspard* — the arrogant know-it-all she'd spent weeks cursing. Now, she had to remind herself of why she disliked him so much.

Just because he was kinder and gentler than she'd thought he would be capable of being, he was still controlling, definitely arrogant and pretty rude to boot. Of course, he had probably spent his life getting his own way on everything, and having people jump to carry out his every command and whim.

Still, for all the advantages he'd been given, he didn't seem uncaring or cold. Instead, she got the sense that he kept his passions tightly leashed and put duty above almost all else. The most important men in her life had devoted their lives to duty. Her father and her fiancé had died protecting and serving their country, and her brother still put his life on the line every day. She could understand where Pierre was coming from, and maybe he wasn't that different from her after all.

She stretched cautiously and let out a low groan at how sore her muscles were. She really did feel like she'd been run over by a Mack truck instead of just having a mild fender-bender with a tree. Well, at least it had been a big tree.

As if summoned by her distress, Pierre tapped on the door before entering. She hid a smile that he'd been thoughtful enough to knock but presumptuous enough to enter anyway before she'd answered.

"You're in pain," he said, frowning. "Take these."

He held out two small, white pills in one hand and a glass of water in the other. She was tempted to argue with his forceful tone, but he wasn't wrong. She *was* hurting again.

She took them. "Thanks," she answered, downing them in one gulp. "I can't believe I slept. How long was I asleep? I can't tell."

"It's mid-afternoon," he confirmed. "I came up earlier to check on you and you were deeply asleep."

She sucked in a quick breath, shocked. "I *never* sleep that long!" she exclaimed. Then, as an afterthought, she realized what a terrible houseguest she was being. Well, not exactly a houseguest, more blizzard refugee meets invader-of-solitude...but still. "Sorry to just...conk out like that again."

"You must have needed it," he said, raising one dark eyebrow, amusement flashing in his eyes. "I think today is the worst you'll probably feel, and the stiffness will likely improve by tomorrow, although it won't go away for a while. I only wish I could do more to take your pain."

His words were intense...and honest. She didn't think Pierre probably said anything he didn't mean, and this didn't seem like just a platitude to be kind. There was a warm melting sensation somewhere in the vicinity of her heart.

"Thanks," she said softly, sincerely. She curved her lips into a wry smile. "Unless you have a masseuse with snowshoes on standby who makes house-calls, I think I'm just going to have to wait this one out." Her laugh fell flat into the silence.

Pierre had an odd expression on his face, almost as if he wanted to say more but had decided not to. Something in her face must have changed his mind, because he answered in an uncomfortable voice.

"It happens that *I* know a number of therapeutic massage techniques."

She raised her eyebrows so fast and high that she thought they might be touching her hairline. "*Really*?" She tried, but she didn't think she did a good job of keeping the incredulity out of her voice.

He narrowed his eyes. "You don't have to sound so shocked," he admonished. "I...well, we all learned when Clothilde was recovering from her car accident. We took turns visiting her, making sure she was feeling better."

The image of Clothilde's brothers, the three tall, handsome, wealthy playboys, learning massage techniques to help their little sister was heartwarming.

In fact, she imagined what it must have cost him — how much he must trust her — to tell her something like that.

"Did you... I mean, you're so busy... Didn't you think of having a professional masseuse come in?"

Pierre sat down heavily on the bed next to her, half-turning toward her so his face was highlighted by the muffled glow of the hallway and giving her a view of his perfectly noble profile. She pulled her knees up in front of her and winced a little at the movement.

"She wasn't..." He sighed, and she noticed little lines around his mouth that she'd never seen before. "She didn't trust anyone. She had already been incredibly sad, devastated by the betrayal of the man she'd loved since childhood. Then when we realized that her horrible accident hadn't been an accident at all, she could barely stand to be around anyone for a while."

"It must have been so awful... No, I won't even say that because 'awful' is too tame a word." She put a tentative hand on his back, feeling the hard muscles bunched there. "I can't even imagine," she finished, feeling like it wasn't enough.

Pierre surprised her when he answered. "Claude was truly like family to us. He wounded us when his relationship with our sister ended so badly, but then, when we discovered he'd been behind the other attacks on our family? There is no way to describe it. Everything we hear about him now, all that has come out since his arrest, seems to paint him as some sort of criminal mastermind, involved in drug trafficking, human trafficking and more. It's —" Pierre went even more rigid, although she didn't know how that was possible. "I ask myself every day how we could have missed his real nature and what a truly sick bastard he is."

Marina moved closer without thinking, unable not to respond to the unmistakable guilt and agony in his voice. She moved her hand along his arm until it rested in his, and he didn't push it away.

"I don't know how you could have been expected to see what he hid from everyone. I mean, from what Annelise tells me, the police had been hunting him for years but had literally no leads. If he hadn't gone after you, he could probably have anonymously continued his illegal business unchecked, basically forever."

Pierre grunted his acknowledgement of her words. "We certainly had invested our own resources, as well, but foolishly didn't see what was in front of our faces. The demon masquerading as a man who we'd let into our homes, our lives... It was *my* job to protect my family, my *sister*, but I failed."

Marina recognized survivor's guilt when she saw it. Heck, she recognized it in her eyes every morning, every time she dared to be happy again.

"So, you helped her recover in any way that you could," she guessed.

He looked back at her fully, appearing surprised at her insight — maybe surprised she was there at all. "Yes, exactly. We wanted Clothilde to feel safe while she got back to feeling whole again, and we could do that for her."

Marina had a sudden stinging in her eyes, but she coughed to cover the intensity of her emotions. That was one of the sweetest things she'd ever heard.

"I'd really like for you to massage me, then, if you're still offering."

Oh, *bon Dieu*, what had he been thinking, offering to massage her beautiful body for any reason? If he was trying to stay away from her — and he told himself again that he was, that he *had* to — this was a hell of a shitty way to do it. At her sweet words, telling him she trusted him to touch her, his cock sprang to attention like a broken jack-in-the-box, straining the front of his trousers with how eager he was to get his hands on her — any part of her, for any reason.

Merde, he was in deep. He couldn't take the offer back now, though. He didn't know why he'd felt comfortable enough to tell her things about their history with Claude that he'd barely shared with his siblings, but it had felt so right, having the warmth of her touch on his back, then her hand held in his. The words had come tumbling out. For a man who controlled every movement, every action, every emotion, she was testing, then just flat-out breaking, his control. Worse, though, he liked it. *Merde*, he *loved* it. He wanted to tell her things, to feel her reaction, to feel her sympathy. He could have sworn he'd felt empathy and understanding practically rising from her pores. Pierre didn't need anyone, ever. But he damn well craved Marina.

"Thank you, *chérie*," he answered, turning fully toward her and holding her gaze.

Her laugh was beautiful, like sunshine. "Why are you thanking me? You're the one offering to give me a massage. I am definitely getting the better end of this bargain, bud."

He shouldn't do it, but he couldn't resist baiting her. He leaned forward, so he spoke close to her ear. "Are you? I'm the one who gets to put my hands all over you."

She shuddered, and he watched the movement with deep satisfaction. She tried for a light smile, but it wavered on her lips. "Hey now, you can just touch me like you touched your sister."

His chuckle surprised him. He felt like he had laughed more with Marina than he had with anyone but his family in years...maybe more than he had laughed, even with his family.

"Ah, *Marinette*. I might use the same movements, but you cannot ask that of me. Touching you will be *nothing* like touching my sister. Now, I need you lying down. I presume you will not agree to strip off your clothes?"

He feared he'd gone too far when she stiffened, but then she quirked one eyebrow up in reproach, her amusement clear.

"Nice try. You assume correctly, as I'm sure you know, *Monsieur* Gaspard."

As she shifted on the bed, he realized that it would be easier with the higher surface of the bed in his room instead.

"Wait." He stopped her with a gentle hand on her shoulder. "I was only half-joking before, *chérie*, but please believe that I have no ulterior motives. However, I realize that this would be more comfortable for both of us in my bedroom instead."

The look she shot him was dubious, but she didn't reject the idea outright.

"I had my bed raised when I was staying here after my injury. I'm a tall man..." He rubbed the back of his neck uncomfortably, realizing that he hadn't meant to reveal so much. Doggedly, he continued. "It was easier to get out of bed that way, but that's not the point. It will be easier for me to reach you, too, and you won't sink into the mattress."

Marina turned fully and placed her hands over his. They felt warm and soft, and the gesture was so kind that he wasn't sure he could stand it.

"Just how badly injured were you, Pierre? Did your family know?"

He looked away, and a dull heat crept up his cheeks. *Merde*, she had him blushing like an errant schoolboy.

"I bet that you downplayed it to them, so they wouldn't worry. Otherwise, they would never have let you come here alone." Marina's guess was so spot on that he felt naked, as though she could see into him in a way that he didn't want or like.

"It was...*difficult*," he acknowledged, the words feeling pulled out of him. "Will you come to my room, then?"

Where before she had hesitated, now she began to rise, gingerly at first, as if the movements were painful. When he stood and reached out to support her, she allowed him to help. He refused to think about how much her acceptance warmed him or how he enjoyed touching her, helping her.

He wrapped an arm around her waist, and his body thrilled at the sensation, but he tried to keep his motions non-threatening. Platonic. *As if that's possible with Marina*, his inner-devil laughed, but he staunchly crushed that thought.

"Just leave me in the powder room for a moment, and I'll meet you there," Marina said, pausing in front of the bathroom door.

He couldn't help the grin that spread across his face. "Are you embarrassed, *chérie*? I never would have expected it of you," he drawled.

Her cheeks flushed pink. "I know that I may seem bold—I *am* in many ways—but I was also raised by a very strict, ladylike grandmother. That sort of thing doesn't just leave you when you grow up."

"I find it charming." He let go of her and turned away. "In fact, I find everything about you more charming than I should," he muttered as he continued toward his room. He thought she wouldn't hear, but her huff of breath made him think that she had. *Merde* again. He was really going to have to be better at hiding his attraction or he would end up going exactly where he'd sworn not to go with her.

As she shuffled her way down the hall toward the room that she assumed was Pierre's—based on the faint sounds coming from it, since she hadn't actually seen it yet—Marina felt conflicted again. She'd decided not half an hour earlier that she should keep her distance from him—well, as much as anyone could keep their distance from someone they were stranded with in a cabin during a blizzard—but he kept on giving her pieces of himself that made her long to break her own resolution. Heck, she felt like she might just know him better after such a short time than she'd known her last four boyfriends, combined. She'd given her virginity to one of them, more to get rid of it than out of a genuine sense of connection, and when he'd been inside her, she had never felt so apart from anyone.

Annelise told her that she kept choosing, either consciously or unconsciously, men who she knew she'd never really fall in love with, so they would never be competition for Jaime in her mind. She had begun to fear that her best friend was right. Most of the time, she accepted invitations from guys who she thought she felt optimistic about, but who turned out to be jerks who droned on about themselves and weren't really interested in her beyond how attractive they thought she was. She knew she was considered beautiful. She would have had to be blind and deaf not to hear that men often appreciated her appearance. But hardly anyone looked beyond the outside shell, and maybe it was true that she felt uncomfortable when they did.

Frankly, Pierre wasn't too far off from the type of man she usually found attractive. He was both physically large, strong and striking, and he could be a bit of an arrogant SOB. Okay, *more* than a bit. But there was certainly greater depth to him than the surface suggested, and the more he revealed, the more she thought she might really grow to like him. She had the uneasy sensation that he saw and heard much more about her than she wanted him to. This time, though, instead of making her run in the opposite direction, she wanted to run toward him.

When Pierre appeared in front of her, though, she felt suddenly certain that she would be safe, that he would take care of everything. In her mind's eye, she ran the short distance to him and he enfolded her in his arms so tightly it was almost painful.

She shook away the disturbing vision, focusing back in on her face in the mirror. *Damn it.* Was she just overtired or was her mind showing her something? She thought she'd long since grown out of anything like that — what her nana had just called 'knowings' — but it had felt incredibly realistic. Although maybe it was just her mind urging her, telling her she could trust Pierre.

She could tell that he was resisting whatever the pull was between them, too. Oddly, that made her feel better about it. He wasn't pushing her. He was darn reluctant, in fact, determined not to get closer. Something about that just drew her right in like a honeybee to nectar, and didn't that make her some sort of messed up?

An imp of mischief popped into her thoughts. *What if I did take off my clothes?* Once the idea surfaced, she couldn't get it out of her head. *It would make the massage better, after all. He suggested it first.* Imagining the shock that would be on his handsome, usually impassive features decided her. It would be worth it to see his consternation alone and to have confirmation of his attraction for her. They would never act on it, but she wanted this—wanted to know how beautiful this one man found her, how badly he wanted her. She stripped down to her panties, grinning in anticipation.

Chapter Six

Pierre had taken the time to get out some of the healing oils that he'd gotten when he'd tried to learn more about massage, and which had helped him as he'd recovered from his own severe injuries. He lined them up in a row, unable to stop himself from making sure they looked perfectly aligned and inhaling deeply to take in the mixture of scents. His sense of smell wasn't what it used to be, but in many ways that had made him more sensitive to scent. He imagined it might be like someone who temporarily lost their sense of sight then was nearly blinded in dim light for a while. His fingers practically twitched to touch Marina.

He spun around at the small sound of her in the hallway, and he thought his mouth actually went slack with shock, which quickly transformed into hot desire.

"W-what are you doing, *bébé*?" he ground out, his voice gone husky and warning. She was absolutely incomparable—stunning beyond words. Her form was tall and lithe, but her hips, butt and breasts were lushly rounded and soft-looking. Her dusky-pink nipples hardened under his gaze, and his mouth went so dry that he thought he heard his breath click.

She flipped her hair over her shoulder, and his cock swelled impossibly harder at the way the motion made her breasts bob slightly.

"I changed my mind…thought I'd be more comfortable with less clothing, after all. It's not a problem, is it?"

He narrowed his eyes, trying to figure out what she was playing at. Hadn't they just agreed, albeit tacitly, that they would keep their hands off each other?

"Oh, I don't mind, *chérie*. If you come a little closer, I'll be happy to show you how much I don't mind, with my hands and my tongue and my cock, shoved so deep inside you you'll never want another man."

Pierre was hoping that by speaking so crudely, he'd scare her away, but instead she gave a delicate shiver. Was it possible she was as into this as he was? It would be too cruel to contemplate, if she were the one woman truly made for him and he had to deny himself…deny them both.

He read the indecision in her eyes, as if she'd planned to tease him but hadn't fully bargained on his response. *Good.* She should know not to play around with men like him. It would be for the best if—no, *when*—she refused. Still, his heart felt like it hung on a razor's edge as she opened those pretty, lush lips of hers. His cock swelled impossibly larger, even as he braced himself for her refusal. He could be a gentleman, no matter how much his body begged him to be otherwise.

Whatever she was going to say was halted in mid-air when there was a large rumble and cracking sound from outside. *Merde*, he realized. The sound had come from where the generator was. There was a sick-sounding gurgle and the lights flickered and died.

Marina's breathing was loud in the sudden silence. "What happened?" she whispered, her worry coming through clearly, even as he could tell she was trying for calm by the deliberately slow breaths she was taking. Her fear was like an icy bucket of water, extinguishing his lust and replacing it with a wave of protectiveness.

"I won't lie to you. I think that was the generator, and it sounded like some sort of storm damage. I can go take a look, but I'm not too hopeful."

She made a sound like a sigh, but with an edge of worry. He could barely make out her form in the premature darkness caused by the storm, but he heard her take a tentative step toward him. He guessed it was probably unconscious, but it was a thrill that she trusted him that much when she was as vulnerable as she must feel, nearly naked in the sudden gloom. He did have the fleeting wish that he could have seen more of her beautiful, sexy body, but now he only wanted to keep her feeling safe. He reached into one of the drawers in the bureau nearest to him to grab one of his softest cashmere sweaters and thick, woven pajama bottoms that would certainly be too long but would keep her warm.

He made his way to her mostly through sound alone and traced his hand lightly down her arm and squeezed her hand before handing her the clothing. "Here, *bébé*. Hate to cover that silky skin—but I want you to be warm, just in case."

"Thanks," she answered, brushing his rough fingers with her softer ones as she took the small bundle. "Do you think it will get really cold in here?" Some trace of waning light from outside caught her eyes and they shone for a second as she pulled on his clothes unquestioningly.

He considered her question. "If I can't repair whatever happened, I would guess it will take overnight for us to really feel more of the cold, but if we stay by the fire, we should still be fine. Let's check out the damage first, though, *hein*?"

She was so close to him — or he was so close to her — that he could feel how shaky her nod was. He couldn't help himself. He reached out to tuck some of her long waterfall of hair behind her ear.

"Whatever happens, we can stay warm enough to survive, and we're in no danger of running out of food. I know enough to take care of both of us for a time, if it comes to that."

She stiffened next to him and he felt her straighten. "I can help take care of us, too. There's no need for you to do it all. I'm more than capable, Pierre." She sounded offended, but he preferred her fire to her fear.

"I never doubted it, *chérie*. I have always thought you were fierce and brave…even before I met you." He coughed to cover up how uncomfortable he was at what he'd inadvertently spoken aloud.

"Let's go now, before it gets any worse. Can you hold the rope by the open door, so I can find my way back?"

When she answered, her voice held resolve, and the sassy attitude that drew him in like nothing else.

"If the Great and Powerful CEO can handle going outside in this mess, I think I can manage to help you avoid wandering off."

Putain, he was in so much trouble when she used that snippy voice.

Pierre has been out there for too long. Or, at least, she was beginning to think so. Time passed slowly, what felt like an hour each minute, as she stood by the door, leaving it cracked open but braced with her foot so it couldn't blow all the way open and let in the thick, swirling mass of snow that howled like a possessed banshee. At first, she'd been able to feel his movements along the nylon rope, but it had gone slack a little while earlier. She'd assumed that he had reached the generator, but now…she wasn't certain.

"Damn it, Pierre," she said out loud, feeling better hearing something other than the storm raging outside. The little light that had been left outside was fading rapidly and it looked like it would soon be nearly full darkness, so that even when there was a break in the swirling snow, she couldn't see more than a foot or two in front of her face. When she flashed the truly enormous flashlight—which Pierre had adorably referred to as a torch—that he had left her with while he took the smaller, more portable one, it just showed her a wall of snowflakes. They were lucky that the banks hadn't built up too high near the side door, or he wouldn't have been able to trudge out there at all.

"Pierre!" she called, but it felt like her words just hit a soft wall and didn't travel. She didn't hear anything in return, and it had been long enough that she was getting genuinely worried. What if he'd slipped and fallen? She'd tried tugging on the rope before and had gotten no answering tug, but she figured she would try again. Trading all the remaining heat for the icy air that came in even through the small crack couldn't be good. This time, when she tugged on the brightly colored flexible nylon rope, which Pierre had told her they used for rock-climbing, there seemed to be even more slack.

With a sick feeling of dread in the pit of her stomach, she realized she didn't feel anything on the other end. She pulled harder then began drawing the limp rope back into the house. As she feared, she was able to pull it all the way in, right to its tattered end. Her heart sank. The rope had gotten severed somehow, and Pierre was out there alone, in a blizzard, with no anchor.

"Shit, shit, shit!" she exclaimed. What had cut the rope? A rock or a sharp object on the side of the house? She prayed it hadn't been something that had fallen on Pierre as well. At the thought of him getting hurt, something dark rose inside her, taking her by surprise. *No.* Every cell in her body rebelled at the thought. He couldn't be hurt. In spite of herself, she was growing to like him. *A lot.* He was not allowed to get hurt, or worse. Not while she was able to do something about it, at least.

Grimly, she looked around, and ran for the front hall closet where she thought she'd seen a long coat hanging. She pulled it out with a cry, relieved that while it was large, it was much thicker than her own, which was still damp from the day before Pierre had already helped her put on thick boots, kneeling at her feet in a way she didn't imagine he would do for many people, but she tightened the elastic at the tops again. She would need all the help she could get, going out into this. She tugged on a hat, scarf and mittens that she found in the bin next to the closet and grabbed another coil of rope.

With the vague idea of information from books she'd read long ago and movies she had seen set in colder climates, she tied the ends of both ropes to different things, one a heavy chest, bench and mirror piece, and the other around a brass sconce on the wall that jutted out a little. When she was sure they were secure, she tied the other ends around her waist, and made sure that the slack wasn't tangled at all. She didn't feel confident in what she was doing, but she knew that she had to do something, and this seemed like the best bet. The longer Pierre was stuck out there, even if he was just inching his way along the outside wall of the house, the more likely he would get hypothermia then become disoriented.

Her sore muscles protested her movements, but she didn't care. She should have been thinking about how important Pierre was to his family, but instead, she was picturing his eyes when he teased her and the rough gravel in his voice when he'd told her what he wanted to do. Even with an icy arctic blast of air blowing into the door, now fully opened, she was warm inside her thick cocoon of clothing. Warmed by her thoughts of him.

She took a deep breath, steeled her nerves and stepped outside. It was so cold that it took the breath right out of her lungs, and even through the scarf that she'd wrapped over her mouth, she had to take shallower breaths. She reached down to feel for the two knots at her waist, and they still felt steady and solid, a talisman in the storm. She stomped and waded through the heavy snow, keeping her hand on the side of the house as she went in the direction Pierre had gone. He'd told her that the generator was on the back wall on the far right corner of the house.

It was hard work, cutting through the snow, and it was difficult to keep her balance since it was heavy and slippery. She felt wet clumps of it sliding down into her boots in spite of how tightly she'd cinched the elastic. Her breath was loud to her own ears, seeming to echo inside of her hood. She scanned around herself after nearly every step, hoping she would see Pierre's tall form in his black winter gear, but all she saw was gray, since the snowflakes looked gray in the dark twilight.

Her stomach felt hollowed out with anxiety by the time she had nearly reached the back corner. *Why haven't I seen him yet? What if he isn't there? What do I do then?* The questions repeated themselves inside her head, and she tried to stay calm and optimistic, telling herself that she would certainly find him at the generator. She finally turned the corner and she almost didn't see him until she was nearly on top of him. In fact, she nearly tripped over him since she was looking around instead of down.

"Oh my God, Pierre!" She crouched down immediately, flashing the beam of her flashlight over the length of his body, the bottom half of which looked like it was covered with part of a tree. There was so much snow that it was difficult to be sure. However, it was clear that a tree had badly damaged the generator, which looked practically smashed.

As she flashed the light back onto Pierre, she saw a bright trickle of red blood on his temple. She took off her right mitten and reached a tentative hand to touch his cheek just above his scarf. It felt icy, and he didn't move a muscle at her touch. She called his name, and gently, then not-so-gently, prodded him, but he remained deeply unconscious. She would have feared he was dead if she couldn't see the blood pumping sluggishly at his temple, and see puffs of his breath rising into the cold storm before it was blown away from them in swirls of snowflakes.

She fought a rising sense of panic. Pierre needed help, immediately, but it would be nearly impossible to drag him back to the door through the storm if he were a dead weight. She couldn't even consider what kind of damage she might be doing to his back if he had any kind of spinal cord injury, because if she left him, he would freeze to death. No help would be able to reach them before that happened, even if they could somehow get through the storm.

Marina sat back on her heels and tried to center herself, finding an anchor in the maelstrom of emotion and worries. She pictured Jaime's face, telling her about how he pushed all the emotions away just before he went into battle. Oddly, though, Pierre's face flashed in front of her eyes and it was more of an effort to imagine Jaime. It felt like forever but was probably only a few seconds until she could see Jaime, and hear him answering her when she had asked him worriedly, so long ago now, how he didn't get distracted when he was in so much danger.

'*Mi corazón*,' he had answered tenderly, brushing a tear from her cheek with one warm fingertip. '*I imagine a box, and I push everything into it and close it up tight until I become pure instinct and training. To do what I must, I can never let emotion enter into it. I can't think of your beautiful face, your worry,* nada. *That is how I make sure I live to come back to you. I know you would too, if you had to.*'

As always, Jaime's words steadied her, and she pushed all her own emotions aside. Her growing feelings for Pierre didn't matter. Her doubts as to whether she was doing the right thing, worry that she might not be strong enough — all that melted away and she was left only with a steel core of resolve. *No man left behind.* She was the daughter and sister of soldiers, and she had been the beloved of another one. She could do this. She had a sudden sense of rightness, a certainty that she would succeed if she could appeal to what mattered to Pierre most.

"Pierre, honey." She shook him gently as she spoke, her words tender but urgent. "You have to wake up. Your family needs you." She paused and bit her lip, thinking about what was truly most important to this man lying in front of her. The possessiveness in his expression as he'd spoken to her earlier had been unmistakable, the drive to care for her. "*I* need you," she added. Incredibly, she heard him groan in response and hope flared like a firecracker inside her. "We have to get back to the house, but I need you to help me. Can you do that?"

His dark eyes flickered open, confused at first but quickly growing determined. She read a fierce protectiveness in his gaze that warmed her from the inside out.

Chapter Seven

Merde, his leg and head hurt like a *fils de putain*... He knew he was confusing his thoughts between English and French, but his mind felt scrambled. Even through the fog of pain and unconsciousness, Pierre felt a sense of urgency, a demand that he couldn't ignore. Someone needed him. No, *she* needed him. *Marina.* In his unguarded state, before he fully returned to consciousness, he recognized what he had been denying, even to himself. There were so many reasons that he shouldn't touch her, shouldn't get involved with her and shouldn't care for her. He would keep to his resolve not to do either, but damn it if she still hadn't wormed her way under his skin, down deep to where he kept his emotions buried. No matter what, he needed to make sure she was safe. He would fight through any pain, any storm — *anything* — just to ensure that her vibrant, beautiful spark wasn't extinguished.

The thought gave him the strength to fully pry open his eyelids, gritty with...ice? *What the hell?* It was...

What was the crazy English expression that he loved? Ah yes, cold as a witch's tit. *Nope, colder.* The face of the woman hovering over him was wrapped in what looked like his brother Luc's scarf, and one of his own hats, so she was barely recognizable, but he thought he might recognize those eyes anywhere. He'd seen them in his dreams often enough, even though he'd tried to stop them. Of course, he hadn't really wanted the visions to end.

"What happened? Why am I lying on the ground?" He tried to be loud, but the wind stole his words away, and his throat felt raw and savaged from the effort. It was almost worth it when she leaned very close, putting her cheek against his to position her ear next to his lips. A strand of her soft hair brushed his forehead, but he was so cold he was surprised he felt it.

"*What…happened*?" he bellowed, but she didn't flinch. Instead, she shook her head and gave an exaggerated shrug. She tugged the scarf under her chin so he could see her mouth to read her lips.

"I think something fell on you…cut the rope." She gestured at her waist, where he saw two ropes tied. He tried to remember how he'd gone from leaning over the generator and assessing the damage, which had looked severe, to lying on the snowy ground. His memories were just too damn foggy.

"Gotta get you back!" Even though he knew she was shouting, he could barely hear her, but her concern came through loud and clear in what he could see of her expression.

He tried to move his leg and a white-hot bolt of pain lanced through it at the motion.

"Hurts." He grimaced. "Stuck under a tree, maybe?"

She nodded her agreement. The way she ran her mitten-covered hand along the side of his face was not something he'd forget anytime soon. It wasn't so much the gentleness of the gesture, which was achingly tender, but the softening in her eyes as she looked at him, obvious even in the dim light only from the torch. It was the way a woman looked at a man she cared for, whether either of them wanted to admit it or not. She had been truly worried about him — was *still* worried.

"Going to try to lift it. Can you try to move when I do?"

He hated that she had to do this, but there was no way he was getting out on his own. It was going to hurt like hell, but if she were willing to haul the tree off him, in spite of her injuries, he could damn well do his part to scramble away.

Nodding made his head throb, but he gritted his teeth against the pain. "Let's do it!" he yelled.

Marina pulled the scarf back up over her face and adjusted her mittens before she scrabbled across the icy expanse of snow. As he saw how small she looked amid the branches of whatever tree had fallen on him — and he would have sworn that none of the large trees were close enough to the cabin to do this much damage — he had second thoughts. There was no way that she would be able to lift it, and she might hurt herself more in the process. He tried to call her back, but he was sure she didn't hear him.

The weight of the branch was heavy on his injured leg, and he knew he must have done something bad to the ligaments in his knee. Then, almost impossibly, he felt a lessening of the pressure on his leg. Marina was shaky, but she had somehow gotten a grip on the tree and was lifting it, although she looked like she wouldn't be able to hold it long at all. He felt a surge of intense gratitude, mixed with something like pride. *Merde*, she was incredible.

He didn't dwell on the thought, though, as he braced himself. He dug the fingers of both hands into the snow and dirt, getting a passable grip. It wasn't great, but it would have to do, as Marina already looked as if her muscles were quaking. With a herculean effort, he pulled himself with all his strength, and dragged his leg out from under the tree. The bark scraped his skin and his muscles burned with the pressure as the trunk and branches marked every place they touched, but his relief at being freed made him weak. Actually, maybe his injuries and being so damn cold made him weak, but he refused to acknowledge that alternative.

He was rewarded when Marina turned back to him and lowered her scarf again, her eyes shining with relief, even as her eyelashes were coated and spiky with ice.

"We did it!" she mouthed. When she began working at the knot that tied one of the ropes around her waist, he couldn't help but notice the frayed end of it. It looked jagged, but also slightly melted. Jagged fit with some rock severing it, and maybe a tree, although it seemed weird. But melting didn't fit. He needed to look at it much more closely. Something seemed off and his instincts were screaming at him, but his sluggish mind couldn't hone in on what exactly was bothering him so much.

Marina reached around him, pressing the fullness of her bosom against his chest and making his breath hitch, even through the thick layers of both of their jackets, recalled him to the present. He was elated, sitting in the snow in the middle of a blizzard, when he should be focusing on how they were both going struggle back inside without freezing to death or hurting themselves — again.

"Thank you, *chérie*," he said, letting his very real gratitude bleed into his words when her face was nearest to his, and he knew she heard by the way her mouth softened.

"Put your arm around my shoulder...lean on me like a big crutch," she directed, her words oddly intimate as she spoke directly into his ear. Then, she suited her words to actions as she maneuvered herself under his arm and they worked together to stand up. He tried to keep the bulk of his weight off her, but he didn't think he succeeded as he grunted with the effort of getting his legs underneath him. When they actually started to rise, it was all he could do not to collapse and slide them back onto the slippery, snow-covered ground.

Marina never faltered, holding steady in spite of the uneven, icy surface and his much-heavier weight. He imagined that her shoulders and leg must be hurting now, too, and he had the fleeting wish that he'd just given her that massage and stayed inside. His estimation of her rose even higher, although with the thoughts he'd been having about her, he wouldn't have guessed that would have been possible. He thought he heard her groan once, but he couldn't be sure.

Finally, they were both standing, and they made their slow, plodding way back along the wall of the house, using the ropes as guides. She'd been resourceful, getting another rope out of the closet as protection in case they got separated. The storm raged on, but it did seem to be slightly less violent than it had been earlier, although visibility was still shockingly low. His knee felt like a twisted mess, but he had lived through excruciating pain before. He could handle this.

Finally—*finally!*—they reached the side door again, and seeing the end so close gave his steps a renewed vigor. They crossed through the large door together, and he reached to slam it closed behind them with a boom that echoed in the cabin.

Marina turned to him and her smile was broad and elated. Then she wobbled and he shot out his hand to steady her, bringing them much closer together.

"Careful," she said in a voice that sounded like a mix between hoarse and husky, probably because of all the yelling they had done. "It's slippery from all the snow blowing in."

He knew he should step back or do something to break the awkward silence, but he couldn't seem to look away from her beautiful eyes. He cleared his throat, and the pain brought him right back to reality.

"We should get off the tiles, *bébé*," he rasped, speaking hurting his voice. It had probably hurt him outside, too, but he'd been too cold and worried to notice. "We can't have one of us slipping and falling again. Another injury might just do us in." His words were darkly humorous, and Marina managed a tremulous smile, but her eyes filled with tears.

"You could have died, Pierre. If I hadn't come out—"

He stopped her from finishing the thought by pulling her into a tight hug, needing to feel her in his arms more than anything else in that instant.

"But you did," he finished. "You came out and saved me, *Marinette*, like some avenging snow angel."

She snorted—a cute little ladylike snort, but a snort all the same.

"*Avenging snow angel?*" she repeated, muffled against his coat. "That's terrible! Did your brain or your eyes get frostbite?"

"Oh, you have no right to criticize. Was that a snort I just heard?"

Marina pulled back enough to look up at him, and his heart squeezed at the sight of the tears on her cheeks, even as she smiled at his teasing.

"I'd like to deny it, but...it's a terrible quirk. My brother called me Piglet for years when we were younger, and Jaime used to crack up every time—"

She stepped back and her eyes shuttered, but not before he saw the pain in them.

"Jaime?" he asked, knowing that her answer was important.

Marina looked away, anywhere but at him. "We should sit down. We need to look at your leg. We'll be lucky if we have two good arms and legs between the both of us, now."

"I'll sit down if you tell me who Jaime is," he answered. The jealous rage he felt shimmering inside of him was an ugly thing, and he knew he shouldn't allow it to seep into his words, but he couldn't stand the softness and love he heard in her voice directed toward another man.

She bit her lip, a nervous gesture of hers that he'd noticed before, and he could practically see her considering refusing. In the end, though, her compassion won.

"Fine, but you're an ass, playing on my sympathy to get your way."

He loved the fire he saw behind her eyes, much more than her tears. *Dieu*, she was a beautiful woman. She unzipped her coat and tore off her hat, revealing a fuzzy mass of staticky waves of hair, but she was still stunning.

"Oh, I am definitely an ass, *chérie*. I never claimed to be otherwise. You'd do well to remember that." He wasn't sure if he was warning her or bragging about it. "Just drop your things on the floor. We'll pick them up later."

She narrowed her eyes but did as he said, just leaving all her outer garments on the floor. It reminded him of how she might look if they got home from an evening out, starting to pull off her clothes at the front door and leaving a trail all the way up to the bedroom. He shook his head to dislodge the fantasy. Why couldn't he seem to keep his mind off sex around her? Especially when she was glaring at him as if letting him strip her naked was about the last thing that she'd allow? He started to take off his coat, but he winced as his hand brushed the zipper.

Instantly, she was in front of him again, cradling his hand in hers.

"Oh my God, Pierre! What happened to your hands?"

He looked down, surprised to notice that both hands were covered with scratches and cuts. Now that he focused on them, the cuts stung, especially as the feeling came back into them fully. Also, when the hell had he taken off his gloves? He crinkled his forehead in thought.

"It must be from how I held on to haul myself out from under that tree, which you so obligingly held up." It felt like the most likely explanation, but somehow, he thought there was more, but he just couldn't remember.

"Let me," she said, nudging his hands away more gently than her brusque tone would have indicated.

She finished unzipping his coat and reached up to slide it off his shoulders, giving him an impromptu hug that his body couldn't fail to react to. Marina quickly pulled off his hat and scarf as well, then stepped away as quickly as she could. Her cheeks were bright flags of pink, and she darted her eyes around the room. Yeah, she'd felt his reaction. He wasn't sorry. In fact, he liked that she'd reacted that way. Such an intriguing combination of sultry temptress and shy virgin. Which was she, really? He thought he might be willing to get frostbite and nearly die of exposure a second time to find out.

"We need to wash you up a bit," she said, the statement sounding oddly sensual in her husky voice.

They staggered together to the kitchen sink, where he soaped and washed his stinging hands in icy water while she wiped away the blood on his head. He hissed in pain at the movements. Of course, the whole process would probably have hurt more if the water were warmer, so he counted himself grateful, but he was still practically swaying on his feet when they finished.

"We should sit down before we fall down, *chérie*," he rumbled, offering her his arm. "And I need to hear about this other man."

Chapter Eight

She really liked the feel of him next to her – no, she *loved* it. The realization was disturbing when it hit her as they walked to the living room. Actually, it was more like limping, but she was so impressed that they had made it that she wasn't complaining.

Years ago, she had recognized that no one made her feel the same level of attraction that Jaime had. It was just a fact, and she accepted it. She found men attractive, sure, but none of them made her pulse speed up or her intimate places clench with need. No other man made her long to get closer, to take him into her arms and her body. She had almost made peace with that, because maybe everyone only got one chance at love in their lifetime and hers had been wonderful. She had been content. The few times she'd forced herself to get close to someone – and the one sexual experience that had been too lackluster to even be called disastrous – she had been left wondering why she had even bothered.

With Pierre, though, from the first instant she'd heard his voice in that darkened room, her body had reacted in a way she'd nearly forgotten. God, he exuded a kind of sexual magnetism that was like catnip to her. Even now, after having been frozen then sweating as they fought their way back inside, he smelled smoky and spicy, like sin personified. She wanted to lick his neck then move lower. She wanted to lean into his hug again as she had in the entryway and never leave his arms. She wanted him to move in her, to claim her.

As soon as they reached the couch, she nearly leapt away from him to put some distance between them. *Get a hold of yourself, Marina*, she chided herself. She'd been about ten seconds from jumping the poor, injured man, for heaven's sake. She stood in front of the enormous fireplace, staring into the flames while she composed herself, trying to look as though she were assessing the fire. She stroked one of the exquisite werewolf sculptures, noting absently that the stone was incredibly smooth, warmed by the huge fire. It felt decadent against her hand.

Pierre cleared his throat and she whipped her head back around to look at him. She saw the direction of his gaze, right at where she was tracing the *loup-garou*'s chest in loving detail, and she snatched her hand away. Pierre raised one eyebrow and he curled his lips into a knowing smirk, looking the furthest thing from a helpless, injured patient as possible.

"Don't let me stop you, *bébé*. Do you want to be alone with him?" he teased. Something about the hint of pride in his voice stopped her.

"*You* made these, didn't you?" she guessed, but she knew the answer already. His reaction confirmed it. He looked stunned that she had guessed, but the truth of his ownership of his work was obvious. He looked at them like a fond father looked at his children. Incredible as it seemed, because nothing she'd ever heard or seen written about him mentioned anything about it, Pierre was definitely an artist. A truly talented one, too.

"A very long time ago," he answered finally, after the silence had stretched almost uncomfortably long.

"If you're capable of making something so special, how could you ever stop?" she asked.

His smile was wry. "Being a CEO, President, Chairman of the Board and—what did you once call me?—billionaire playboy. Those are all full-time jobs, *chérie*."

"How could your family let you stop using a gift like this? You obviously love these, and it must have taken years of study and practice to learn to carve stone like this."

Pierre shrugged, and the firelight danced on his face so that his eyes were dark in the shadows cast between flickers.

"My brothers and sister were young. Luc and Clothilde barely remember, and Rémy had to give up a great deal, as well. Our parents were—" He paused, as if searching for exactly the right word. "They were self-absorbed, but it wasn't out of neglect. They were just that deeply in love. There wasn't always much room for anyone besides the two of them in their life, but when our mother got sick then passed away, our father just disappeared. Someone had to take charge, and it had to be me. There was no one else."

Marina could hear the determination in his voice—and also the sorrow. He had done it and taken over, but what had it cost him to become Pierre Gaspard? He was harsh and demanding because he had to be, deeply protective and loving toward his family.

"How old were you?" she asked.

"I was nineteen when I made those. I had been taking serious art courses for years and was studying art in college. I was twenty-three when I took over Gaspard Industries."

For such an intensely private and protective person, she knew that he was giving her something he gave few others.

"Do they know what you gave up?" she asked.

His features looked harsh in the low light, and she thought maybe she was seeing the side of him that was a ruthless conqueror in business.

"I don't *want* them to know. I love them. They deserve happiness." His words sliced through the air like a warning, but she was growing to know better than to only hear what he wanted her to.

"And you don't?" she countered.

His gaze was level, and he watched her for a long moment. She stood, unflinching, for his perusal.

"We should build up the fire again," he said at last, moving to stand up.

"No, no…please. You need to rest that leg more. I'm feeling okay. Just tell me what to do and I'll manage," she insisted.

His expression softened. "You really are a city girl, hm? I just need to put a few more logs on, but they need to be positioned right. Even this withered husk of a man can manage that, but I appreciate your offer, *bébé*." He looked considering. "I don't think we remembered to reset the alarm, though. Thank God Villiers and Marc set it to have battery-operated backup, unlike our higher-tech and more automated systems in the other houses, so it should work for another few days at least. The generator was really smashed up even worse than I would have expected was possible. It was like that tree pulverized it with an industrial-sized baseball bat."

"Of course I'll set it," she answered. She couldn't believe they'd forgotten, but understandably, they'd been distracted. And obviously, the door had been open the entire time they had both been outside. The idea made her uneasy, but she dismissed the thought as ridiculous. No one else could possibly be outside in this blizzard. *They* had barely survived being outside in it.

Pierre's expression was dark, then pained, as he struggled back to his feet and went to the iron log rack that held a decent supply of firewood—but not nearly enough for their purpose. "You know what? Could you also enter another code for me? It will put the system into lockdown mode. I just… I'd feel better. Lately, no one but Marc and I have the current code to disarm it, and we change it daily,. Once it's armed, it activates every sensor, and if anyone or any large thing touches a door or window, interior or exterior, it will give us a loud warning." He told her a code that sounded like a date around twelve years earlier.

Marina paused on her way to the door. "Of course," she answered immediately, torn between feeling happy that he trusted her so much and worried that he was feeling the same nagging sense of something wrong. "I can feel it too… Something feels off." She gave a dry laugh. "I mean, apart from being trapped alone together in a blizzard with a broken generator, wrecking my car and having you almost freeze to death after being nearly crushed by a tree."

Pierre nodded slowly. "Come right back, *chérie*. It makes sense for both of us to stay close to the fire, now that we know we won't be getting the power back any time soon. We lost a lot of heat through the door, too."

She rushed as fast as her still-sore muscles would allow. When she reached the entryway, she saw that they must not have closed the door all the way. Weird, because she thought she remembered pushing it closed, but maybe the wind had blown it open? She pushed it all the way closed until she heard the click of a latch, then hastily entered her code, as well as the code Pierre had given her. The control pad blinked bright red three times and gave a long, ominous beep, before going solid red and showing 'Lockdown Mode' in the display.

When she got back to the living room, Pierre was prodding the logs with one of the iron fireplace tools that she had always seen but had never used herself.

"All good?" he asked. Her mouth went dry at how sexy he looked, rugged and masculine and like the thing of deep woods fantasies.

"Yeah, it's definitely armed now. It says, 'Lockdown Mode'."

Pierre nodded. "Good. Do you want some tea, *chérie*? Maybe with a splash of whiskey? The stove is propane—no gas line out here—so it should still be working fine. The propane is right under the counter, so nothing in the storm will have damaged it."

"Tea sounds amazing, but..." She bit her lip, then stopped herself. She had to stop doing that. She tugged at the hem of her shirt instead, which probably wasn't much better. "*You* drink tea?"

Pierre smiled and his teeth flashed white against his tanned skin. "I am a man of many surprising appetites, *bébé*."

She snorted again with surprised laughter and he chuckled in reply, the rich sound bouncing off the high ceilings of the room. The look he shot her was unguarded, and he looked almost boyish, but there was heat there, too.

"You are not at all what I thought after we first met," she blurted out, then fled before she could see his reaction.

When she returned with large cups of tea—laced liberally with whiskey, because why the hell not?—Pierre was sitting down again. He had somehow adjusted the couch so that it had an enormous two- or three-person-sized footrest, and there was a huge, thick comforter lying next to him in a fluffy pile.

"Where did that come from?" she asked.

He raised one dark eyebrow. "We have many secrets at *Chez Gaspard*," he answered mysteriously. She loved this playful side of him. It made him seem lighter and kinder but didn't take away from his dark appeal one bit.

She gave him a skeptical stare.

"There are hidden compartments in the couch, and some of them always have blankets. It gets damn cold here in Vermont," he admitted. "Come sit down. We need the tea so you can fulfill your end of our bargain. We can wrap up and stay warm by the fire."

She handed him one of the mugs, which he sniffed with surprise then a grin, obviously at the strong alcoholic smell, then she settled down next to him in the spot he patted on the couch cushion next to him.

"I like the way you make tea, *bébé*," he rumbled in his husky voice.

She thought about staying apart from him. Just because she was sitting next to him, she didn't have to sit *right* next to him, did she? But then she decided that she didn't care. He could have died, she could have died… The house was going to cool off soon and frankly, she wanted to be next to him. Not just to share body heat—although damn, he was hot—but because she was wildly attracted to him. She wanted whatever she could have with him. From this moment on, she was going to make the most of this interlude and not think about the future.

His face registered surprise then a flattering, hot interest when she climbed up and settled close to him so that she was practically curled into his side. His breathing increased, but she wouldn't have been able to tell if she hadn't been so close to him. He leveled a questioning glance at her.

"We're trying to conserve heat, aren't we?" she answered innocently.

"Indeed," he answered, his tone amused, and he covered them with the thick comforter. It was soft and heavy, and she was safe and warm after the insane worry of finding him lying unconscious on the ground with the rope severed outside.

"*D'accord*, the alarm is set, the fire has been fed and we have nothing more to do until the storm lets up, apart from staying warm together. No more excuses. I believe you made me a promise."

Marina sighed.

"It was a promise made under duress," she countered.

He raised his eyebrows. "I'm an effective negotiator."

She gave a surprised laugh. Yep, the teasing side of Pierre really got to her like nothing else, she thought, although 'brooding and darkly sexy' was also pretty awesome. Hm, maybe she liked most of the sides of him.

"Masterful," she agreed dryly. "However, I believe I'm owed something in return."

"A boon?" he asked.

She smiled knowingly. "Oh no, wouldn't you just love it if I asked for a kiss?"

He bumped her lightly with his shoulder and looked down at her, his eyes seeming to sparkle in the firelight, but with the barely leashed heat of desire.

"I would love that very much, yes," he agreed, his lips twitching as though he wanted to smile but was fighting it.

"I want truth for truth. For every truth I tell you, you have to give me one in return."

Pierre's expression darkened. As he looked at her, she saw suspicion and caution warring with something else — maybe something like hope. She waited him out, refusing to answer first or to back down. If she was going to relive any part of her extremely painful past — the past that she never spoke of, even though she thought and dreamed of it every day — then he would have to give her something in return.

"This is not... I don't give this type of trust...*ever*," he finally admitted. "I did so twice in the past and it...did not end well."

She covered his hand with hers, the gesture such an unconscious expression that she didn't realize he might not like it until he stiffened at her touch. She wasn't sorry, though.

"I don't talk about Jaime, *ever*. I rarely say his name. But maybe I should, and maybe it won't hurt you to share some piece of yourself with me, too." Her words were low and earnest. "I can't trust you with this part of me if you don't trust me with some part of yourself."

The silence hung in the room, making the air feel heavy, but finally Pierre answered.

"Agreed, then, *Marinette*. Truth for truth, but *only* for you."

His words were so quiet that she barely heard them, but she did and her heart soared. It had been important to her, more important than she realized, that he meet her halfway.

"Thank you," she whispered. She closed her eyes and took a deep breath, and the picture she saw in her mind was the photo they'd taken right after she and Jaime had gotten engaged. It was one of her favorites because he'd looked so elated. They'd both felt so very certain of their future together. Of their future, period.

When she opened her eyes again, she was looking at the fire, but her mind had gone far away.

"I don't remember a time when I didn't know Jaime. He was one of my brother's friends, and we grew up together. Eduardo wasn't mean like other older brothers, partly because after our parents died when we were young and we went to live with our nana, we needed each other. When he and Jaime played pirates or fairy tales or even video games, they included me. Jaime loved to pretend to be a knight." She broke off, seeing his boyish face in her mind's eye, fake sword raised above his head as he pretended to slay a dragon or other hideous monster. The memory hurt her heart but made her smile at how fierce he'd been. How positively certain of right and wrong.

"I suppose he never grew out of wanting to save the world," she mused. "Jaime was a sweet boy, kind and gentle, and he always had a soft spot for me. We would play jokes on each other and laugh and talk for hours. He made me feel like the most interesting girl in the world."

Pierre stayed quiet, letting her talk, while the logs crackled in the fireplace, accompanied by the dull roar of the howling wind that was muted by the thick walls, windows and doors.

"As we grew older, he got tall and handsome and I started to notice him in a different way. He started to notice me, too. Our friendship just kind of naturally turned into romance, then love. We had the blessing of his parents, and my nana and my brother, and Jaime courted me. We went to movies and high school dances, the county fair and beach bonfires. He was my world, and I think I was his. He and Eduardo had always talked about joining the Marines after they graduated from high school, so it wasn't a surprise when they did, although—" Her voice caught on the words. "Knowing what I do now, of course I wish things had gone differently. But back then, I was fiercely proud and supportive of them." She turned to look up at Pierre. "I'm still fiercely proud, *always*, but...it's not the same." She didn't know if she was conveying her meaning well, but he nodded.

"It changes you when someone you love dies, and it's complicated further if you don't have somewhere to put your anger."

His insight surprised her, but it shouldn't have. Pierre Gaspard had suffered, and he'd hidden it even from his own family.

"Before he left, Jaime gave me a promise ring. I know that when they join the service, a lot of young guys get some freedom and start making money and they go a little crazy, sleeping with base bunnies and going out drinking whenever they have leave, but I honestly think Jaime didn't even notice anyone else. Eduardo used to complain about it, that he was stuck with a friend who lived like a monk. Jaime wrote or called whenever he could, and he saved every dollar that he didn't send home to his parents to help take care of his younger siblings because he told me he wanted to be able to buy nice things for me and our future children."

A tear rolled down her cheek and her throat tightened. "I always answered that I didn't need nice things. I just needed *him*." She couldn't look at Pierre, but he squeezed her hand.

"He was lucky to have you, *chérie*." His voice was even gruffer than usual.

She took a shaky breath.

"Well, I don't know if you'll still say that when you hear what comes next," she answered. Pierre's expression was unreadable in the flickering firelight when she darted a glance up through the thick veil of her lashes.

"If this is too difficult, you don't have to continue." Pierre squeezed her knee gently with one massive hand, the gesture oddly tender. "I think I may be able to guess what comes next."

"Thanks, but I made you a promise. And I don't think you can guess all of it." Marina didn't know what compelled her, but something inside her ached to tell him things she'd never told anyone, not even Annelise. She wanted him to know *her*, the real her, good, bad and very ugly. The deep need took her by surprise, but it shouldn't have. Maybe, if he didn't turn away from her, she wasn't as terrible as she feared.

"I want to hear anything you have to say, *Marinette*, *always*," Pierre answered simply, and his reply gave her the strength to continue.

"On his second-to-last leave, Jaime proposed, and it was wonderful. Sublime. Everything I'd ever dreamed of. I'll never forget the smell of the ocean that night, the sound of the waves or the feel of his arms holding me, the wonder of him cherishing me. We had a special dinner to celebrate with our families and Annelise took pictures and we thought we would have a wonderful forever love." She shifted position, unconsciously curling closer to Pierre.

"Sometimes, over the years, I've thought that I exaggerated it in my memory or that I imagined it altogether—that spectacular week filled with joy and dreams—but the pictures prove that it really happened. I was that girl, so in love and loved in return, and I didn't even realize how lucky I was."

"That doesn't sound so bad, *chérie*." Pierre's tone was careful, cautious.

Marina shook her head. "Everyone knows about that leave. All our friends and family members were there, and we celebrated together. But there was another leave before Jaime was deployed. He managed to wangle one last weekend. It wasn't even a whole weekend, only thirty-six hours. He came to me right away. I think Eduardo must wonder why I've never mentioned it, but he's never asked." She stopped speaking and nearly decided to leave it at that, her courage quailing in the face of actually confessing what a bad true love and fiancée she'd turned out to be.

"Why *haven't* you mentioned it to anyone else?" Pierre prodded as the silence grew long again.

"The visit started off well, but then…I *ruined* it. He surprised me in the middle of doing homework for my first college classes, and we had the house to ourselves, because my nana was at work. We were kissing on the couch and, you know, cuddling…"

Pierre chuckled. "I know the kind of cuddling."

Marina gave a watery smile. "Then I asked him — no, *begged* him — to make love to me. I said that we were engaged and in love, and I wanted to do everything with him." She blurted it out in a rush, her mouth nearly fumbling over the words.

"This sounds like a dream to me, my *Marinette*," Pierre answered with more gentleness than she would have previously thought him capable of.

More tears fell as Marina forced herself to continue. "I thought so, but he refused. He was…deeply religious. My nana always took us to church, but his parents were even more devout, and he was a true believer as well. He thought it was really wrong. We argued, and I was upset. He promised he would look into moving up the wedding date to as soon as possible, and he told me that he wanted me more than anything." Her chest shook with the force of her tears, and she struggled to get the words out.

"I was humiliated, even though he'd been gentle about it, and I yelled at him to leave — that he should just go back and that I would rather be alone. And do you know what he said? He said that he loved me and always would, and nothing would ever change that." She drew her knees up closer to her chest and put her face into them.

"He left, then four months later he was killed by accidental friendly fire during an ambush. And the last words I ever spoke to him were in anger and embarrassment."

She felt like her ugly confession, of how petty she had been, hung there in the air like a dark cloud.

"You never told anyone? Never talked about this with your brother?" Pierre asked softly.

Marina shook her head, the lump in her throat feeling too large to speak around. "No." She forced out the whisper.

What must Pierre be thinking of her now? He knew she wasn't careful about talking about Annelise with strangers, she'd been really forward with him and now she'd confessed that she'd practically sent the love of her young life, the man she had promised to marry, fleeing out into the night after she'd all but jumped him. The thoughts raced around her head and she almost regretted telling Pierre, but then the same impulse that had prompted her in the first place resurfaced. Pierre Gaspard wasn't perfect, by any means, and neither was she, and maybe he of all people could understand her deep regrets and extra pain.

"*Bébé*—" he began, taking her hand into his, which was rough and injured from whatever he had been doing outside. Without warning, and surprising even herself, she cut him off, suddenly wrung dry from the emotional outpouring.

"Don't say anything now." She heard the pleading note in her own voice, and she hated it but felt powerless to stop it. He opened his mouth again, and she had to stop him.

"Please," she said, more desperately. "I just... I don't have the strength to hear whatever you have to say," she confessed.

He surprised her in turn by gathering her close into the side of his body, protectively.

"For you, then, *chérie*, I will just hold you."

She turned her face into his sweater and inhaled the warm, fresh scent of him, detergent and cologne and sweat. With a clarity that struck her hard between the shoulder blades, she knew that she would gladly stay here, curled next to him with her head on his shoulder, for an eternity. The realization freaked her the heck out and made her feel such a deep conflict that it felt as if her soul might be ripping down the middle.

"Oh, no, *monsieur*. You made me a promise." She tried for a light, teasing note, but it fell flat. Like a gentleman, Pierre ignored it and played along.

"A promise, hm?"

She nodded, loving the softness of his cashmere sweater caressing her cheek.

"I showed you at least three of my demons. I think you owe me some of yours in return."

Chapter Nine

Pierre wasn't certain what the unfamiliar sensation in his chest was—besides damned uncomfortable, of course—but then it hit him with startling clarity. Humbled…he felt utterly humbled and honored by the trust that Marina had shown him in telling the truth about her relationship with Jaime. He hated that she'd been walking around for years feeling guilty, never allowing anyone to help ease the burden. He would honor her wishes and not say anything more about it, but he could damn sure give her something of himself—something he seldom gave to anyone—in return.

"Far be it from me to renege on a promise." His attempt at a light tone fell almost as flat as hers had, but she gave him a tired smile and that made it worth it.

"What do you want to know, *mademoiselle*?"

She absently traced the line of his forearm through his sweater, and he fought the urge to lean into her innocent touch.

"*Everything*." She laughed. "But start with why you, someone who, at least on the surface, has everything he could want or need, has been secretly running to stay at this lodge, and also doesn't seem to like people very much."

His gut churned, but he wasn't sure if it was more because he'd trained himself to never — *never* — share certain parts of himself, with anyone or because he dreaded telling her about the sometimes-difficult past that had shaped him. She squeezed his forearm and it felt more like a caress.

"If you really don't want to talk about whatever it is, you don't have to."

He knew what it must have cost her curiosity to say it, and he loved that she made the offer. He sighed.

"You ask everything and nothing, *bébé*, and you don't even know it." He gave a dry laugh. "As you said, though, a promise is a promise, and I will try to do this for you." His voice roughened, his throat still sore from their earlier shouted conversation. "Again, this is *only* for you."

He'd thought she wouldn't notice, but he should have known better by now. She was an extremely observant woman, and fiercely compassionate, as well as intelligent, something he'd known even just from reading the summary of the detailed background checks Marc had helped him run on all his future sister-in-law's close associates.

"Are you okay? It seems like your throat hurts…was maybe hurting even before?" He didn't miss that she phrased her observation as a question.

"You should have been an interrogator, *chérie*, although I suppose you do research for a living." He took a deep breath and plunged into one of his most carefully guarded secrets. "Yes, I'm okay, although my throat is painful. The full truth is that it was injured very badly about seven months ago now, along with my lungs and my body in general. The accident and illness I was recovering from was an attempt on my life... Well, we're not certain if it was meant to target me or Rémy and Clothilde also. Whatever the intent, though, it nearly killed me. Claude nearly killed me."

"What happened?" Marina asked, concern heavy in her voice.

"Poison," he answered, and he heard her sharp intake of surprise. "In my coffee, one evening at our favorite restaurant after dinner with my brother and sister... Thankfully, I had swift and expert treatment. My physicians told me it was touch and go for a bit, but with an amazing medical team, I was home within a week under close supervision."

She turned her face up toward him and he couldn't help but admire the way the firelight played off the soft curves and angles of her cheeks, highlighting how pink they had become with the warmth of the fire and the blanket. Her eyelashes were still spiky from her crying.

"How could your family leave you alone, knowing how close they came to losing you?" The righteous anger in her voice warmed him, but he had to disabuse her of her perception of his family.

"I didn't only keep my recovery a secret. I also kept the severity from my family entirely. I forced my physicians to give them false information." He knew he sounded clipped, but telling anyone the truth was uncomfortable.

"But *why*?" she asked, shaking her head. "Why wouldn't you want their help?"

He started to answer back by instinct, but then paused, really considering her question.

"Honestly, I think it is a combination. My whole life, I have protected my siblings, our staff, all the people in the sphere and under the protection of my family's name and company."

He loved the crinkle that appeared between her beautifully arched eyebrows, and he wanted to kiss it.

"Why would you have to do that, though? You should have been cherished, protected, spoiled."

"Fair question. The answer is…complex, and it goes back further in the past than you might think." He shifted to get more comfortable, and Marina cuddled more deeply into his side, making something tender and unfamiliar well up inside him.

"I was loved. Our parents truly loved me and my brothers and sister. As I told you before, though, they were deeply in love with each other, utterly devoted. Our father always was a dreamer, too. He probably never would have gone into business, certainly not as the head of a company, if it hadn't already been in our family, with him the only child of wildly successful entrepreneurs and innovators. He had bouts of extraordinary inspiration and innovation, but his closest friend and long-time vice-president, Jean-Marie, Claude's father, was always there to take care of the actual business end of things."

Marina nodded. "I remember you mentioned this a little bit, although everything you read about Gaspard Industries makes your father and grandfather both sound, well, like larger-than-life business geniuses."

Pierre's grin surprised him. "You've been reading up on us? On me?" he asked teasingly.

Marina's cheeks flushed and her gaze shifted, and his heart did an odd stuttering. She *had* been researching him.

"Not on you, just, um, your family, which includes you." She bit her lip, and the gesture was endearing. "I mean, obviously, you're the head of the family, so you were in more articles and pieces—and a surprising amount of online gossip page things with a fair number of interchangeable models as your dates to a whole crapload of charity events and stuff."

He raised his eyebrow. "You looked at pictures of me? You surprise me, Ms. Lopez."

She flushed an even darker shade of pink, and he took pity on her.

"They were geniuses, for sure, but my grandfather was the real business whiz, as well as innovator. My father was just…" Pierre drifted off, still wrestling with the duality of his love for his kind, brilliant father and his ongoing frustration at the total lack of practicality and common sense the man had shown. It was something that Pierre still dealt with the consequences of on a daily basis. "He was fantastically intelligent—and also totally impractical. He got worse, much worse, after my mother passed away. We had to hide it, so I'm not even sure if Rémy, Luc and Clothilde know as much about what he was really like, because we put up a different public face for investors and competitors."

He took another sip of his strong tea and Marina nearly hid a yawn, but he could feel the way her shoulder rose and fell, since they were sitting so close. He raised one sardonic eyebrow, and she looked sheepish.

"I'm so sorry… I want to hear everything, every last word, but I think that being truly warm again and feeling safer…"

She trailed off and he finished the sentence for her. "Combined with this very fine tea you made, *chérie*. I'm feeling pretty drowsy myself."

Marina's staying hand on his chest stopped whatever else he might have said.

"*Please* go on, though. I really want to know all about your past and how it affected your future. Everything about you is interesting to me, Pierre."

When he glanced down at her again, her hair was rumpled but silky-looking in the soft light, and her eyes were an unusual mix of sleepy, intrigued and embarrassed by what she'd revealed. His heart flipped over in his chest. *Bon Dieu*, she was lovely, even like this. *Especially* like this. She had no idea just how beautiful she was.

"*Bon, alors*… I will continue, but I have been warned and I won't be offended if I start to hear you snoring. I'm not really all that fascinating, *chérie*, just wealthy and powerful." His tone was wry.

She shook her head, making her shiny hair nearly sparkle around her shoulders. "You might think that, but I see someone who has deep loyalty and love for his family and his employees, those he considers his dependents. I think that's deeply admirable."

He wanted to dismiss her words, innocent and naïve as they were, but he couldn't. In spite of his efforts, she had gotten under his skin and her opinion mattered more than he wanted it to.

"I don't know about that. The full story — shortened version — is that soon after my father died, the Board of Directors, led by Jean-Marie, gave me an ultimatum.

They knew that I'd been running the company in my father's stead for years, in spite of my young age, but that I had planned to take a different direction, to return to art school and pursue those studies. Several of them saw their chance to combine their voting rights with Jean-Marie's to implement changes and seize true control of the company, so they offered me a buyout."

His gut churned at the memory, of the terrible realization that on that day, either he would be abandoning Gaspard Industries or he would be abandoning his aspirations. The two could not continue to coexist.

"A buyout doesn't sound like such a terrible thing, if you didn't want to run the company. You must have been young, since I read you've been CEO for over twelve years."

Pierre was impressed again at her insight.

"I was elated, at first. I trusted Jean-Marie's advice, just as my father had, and it would have been an extraordinarily profitable deal for our family. On the surface, it appeared that we would retain some input, too, with two Board seats. One of the other long-time Board members shared some additional information with me, though, about the future plans they had presented to select members in secret, for restructuring, major cut-backs and layoffs in some sectors — and an increased focus on weapons."

Marina drew in a harsh breath. "But you don't make weapons, do you?"

Pierre shrugged. "Not as such, but our technology can be implemented in a number of different ways. Outside entities have been known to leverage some of our systems for defense. This plan included an initiative to make better offensive weapons, too. It wasn't a bad idea, either, if that was something you don't have a problem with."

"And you did?" she asked quietly.

Pierre sighed and grimaced when he moved his knee wrong. The pain had already improved, though, so he was hopeful that he hadn't injured it as badly as he'd feared. Still, it was a unique kind of torture to talk about such painful things from his past while trying to ignore the tenderness in his knee and his throat in the moment.

"I tried to keep an open mind—the world needs weapons, too, for the good guys to use—but it bothered me. Gaspard would become a name affiliated with destruction and war, and that would be the legacy left to my brothers and sister without a bit of input from them. Even more, though, thousands would lose their jobs. Those at the top, including me, would profit handsomely, but the rank-and-file employees would be out of work, some with highly specialized skills that might not be transferable in the areas where they have made their homes and brought their families."

"Why couldn't you just refuse the buyout?"

It was a good question.

"The only way for me to truly overrule them was to fully take the helm of Gaspard Industries. As a Gaspard, if I became CEO and Chairman of the Board—and won over the rest of the Executive Board and Board of Directors—I had enough support to restructure on my own terms and remove them. It would be a grueling, thankless task for someone like me, who was widely perceived as a frivolous playboy. I had been helping out in my father's stead, sure, but they banked on my not wanting to go all-in and give up essentially everything else." He took a deep breath, and his voice when he spoke again was ice-cold steel. "They were wrong."

"So you threw yourself into the company, and you obviously won," Marina finished for him, and her voice held a mixture of respect and regret.

"I did," he confirmed.

"Why didn't you tell them, though? Your siblings would have helped you, wouldn't they?"

Pierre frowned. "They did help me... They continue to help me. Being born into our family business is both an astronomical blessing and also a heavy burden. I didn't want them — in fact, I *never* want them — to have anything extra to carry from guilt that by some quirk of nature I was born first and they weren't, so I was the one who had to sacrifice. Any one of them would do the same. In fact, Luc loves the business and PR side of things."

Marina was silent for a long moment. "What happened to Jean-Marie? I thought that Claude was like family and engaged to your sister until relatively recently."

Pierre felt the cold wave of rage well up inside of him at the memory of how Claude had attacked his sister, him, then his brother Rémy. He also felt the familiar prickle of deep discomfort, almost self-loathing, that he hadn't seen how unstable their friend had obviously become. Driven mad by hatred for them...by jealousy.

"Jean-Marie...well, he seemed to take the whole thing pretty well. He was disappointed, sure, and he disagreed with me at first, but once it became clear that I was set on my course, he acted like it was a gamble that hadn't paid off, just business. The couple of times we spoke about it afterward, he treated it like a difference of opinion. I guess I'll never know the truth, but I honestly think he might have thought he would be doing me a favor to help me get out, and he just didn't have the same reservations about making weapons." At the time, Pierre remembered being relieved when his father's closest friend had continued to attend every family birthday and holiday party, since he would have missed the older man he'd loved almost like an uncle.

"We remained close, friendly inside and outside of work, then he left amicably about a year later to form his own company, financed from his cashing out all his shares of Gaspard Industries. I was truly saddened — we all were — when he was killed in a plane crash in the Middle East as he traveled for his new venture, and the company went under pretty quickly without him as the driving force. Claude inherited a decent amount, but nowhere near what he would have had with either his father's shares of Gaspard Industries or the fortune that his father had poured into the new company without ever living to reap the benefits. With just a fortune and no company, he didn't have anything like the respect and power his father had." Pierre squeezed the bridge of his nose, feeling the ghost of sadness he still experienced at the loss of a man who had been like family.

"Apparently, from the little we've learned since he has been imprisoned, Claude blamed our family for his father's death and the significant decrease in their family's fortune. Even while he romanced my sister, dating then asking her to marry him, he was plotting against us."

Pierre stared into the flames, unseeing, remembering how formally Claude had treated

Clothilde. At the time, they'd all thought his attitude was out of respect and devotion to his childhood sweetheart, but in fact, he'd been controlling, emotionally abusive and unfaithful. Still, those horrible flaws paled in comparison to the criminal enterprises he'd undertaken, even while he was planning his wedding to Clothilde.

"I know that Clothilde broke things off when she found out Claude had been cheating on her."

Pierre raised both his eyebrows in surprise. "If Clothilde told you that, she must really like and trust you."

Marina tilted her head to one side. "I know you might not agree, but I *am* generally considered likeable," she teased, pursing her lips. "We've had a couple girls' outings, since that delightful soiree at the Mount Valder. I think Annelise is working her way around to asking us to be her bridesmaids. Also, your sister really can't hold her tequila."

Pierre gave a bark of laughter. "My sister would never drink tequila. She's a wine and champagne girl, with the occasional cognac."

Marina raised her eyebrow and nodded knowingly. "That is exactly what she wants you to think…what almost everyone thinks. But your sister is definitely a free spirit who enjoys her margaritas with salt on the rim."

Pierre shook his head emphatically. "No…I'm sorry, but no. She's wonderful, and I love her, but the most free-spirited thing Clothilde has done is wearing white after Labor Day. It was in all of the American society rags." Still, something about Marina's words made him stop and give the idea some real consideration.

"Although she *has* always had the most wicked sense of humor of all of us."

Marina chuckled. "She looks haughty and unapproachable, but she's a real sweetheart who loves to laugh at the absurdity of your rarified 'Society'."

Pierre was stunned at the accuracy of her observation. "You're totally correct, but no-one ever sees that. She's so shy."

Marina shrugged, but he could tell she was pleased. "I like people. And Clothilde is easy to like, if you just look below the surface a tiny bit." Her expression darkened at whatever she must have been thinking, and he could swear she growled. "That asshole Claude is even worse than Annelise's ex, Kyle, and that prick was a piece of work, let me tell you. Claude takes the cake, though. It was horrible enough that he tried to kill Clothilde and Rémy, but now I find out that he nearly killed you too. I'm glad he's locked up!"

Her chest rose and fell with the force of her emotions, and her passionate response on his behalf pleased him on a deeper level than it should have. But still…

"Did you just growl?" Pierre asked, the question slipping out before he could stop it.

Marina narrowed her eyes. "Maybe," she acknowledged. "Do you have a problem with that?"

Pierre raised one dark eyebrow, looking intrigued. "Will you growl at me again if I answer yes?"

She slapped her hand lightly onto his upper arm, a minor touch, but he winced and her expression of mirth instantly transformed into concern. "I'm sorry!" she said, rubbing his arm gently in a way that made another part of him flare to painful attention as well. Not that his cock had ever truly been at rest around her, but the way she was rubbing his arms so slowly made him think of how he'd like to have her, on her knees, rubbing a different part of him with the same tender attention.

"What happened out there?" she asked.

Pierre searched his memory, but it was still foggy. Well, snowy, really. He shook his head and winced again.

"I'm not sure... I was looking at the generator, thinking I might be able to fix part of it, then there was just pain and gray." No matter how he strained, he couldn't remember more. "I don't know how I wrenched my knee or shoulder—or how I got all scratched up. The next thing I really remember is you...telling me... Did you say you needed me?"

He looked at her questioningly, his voice deepening at the recollection. God, the idea of her saying that to him made some primal instinct inside him stand up and puff out its chest.

She wouldn't quite meet his eyes, and her cheeks went back to the beautiful rosy flush he'd admired before. "It seemed like the only thing that might get you to wake up," she hedged.

"But was it true?" he prodded, watching every flicker of emotion in her expression. She was quiet for so long that he thought she wouldn't answer, but he should have known that Marina would be honest. She was innocence and candor, bold and sweet.

"It was true then, and I think it might be even more true now," she admitted quietly.

He leaned closer, but a loud thump from somewhere inside the house, followed by a blaring siren, made him freeze.

Chapter Ten

Almost as soon as the alarms started shrieking, Pierre shot to his feet, making all his muscles scream in protest. He pushed the pain and all other distractions aside, blocking everything but his focus, as he let all his classes and training from his youth take over. He reached down into another drawer in the couch, separate from the one that held the blankets that he and Marina had been nestled under, and put his thumbprint on the specially-coded box without needing to look, having rehearsed this maneuver until it was smooth and fluid.

He dimly heard Marina suck in a sharp, shocked breath as he lifted the compact pistol to his side and flipped off the safety.

"What was that noise? Why do you have a gun?" she asked, and he hated the quaver in her normally-strong voice.

"Just a precaution, *chérie*. I think I'm just on edge from earlier. It's probably nothing, but—" he debated how much to say and landed between reassurance and total honesty. "Something about what happened outside has my—what do you say?—Spidey senses going off like crazy. If you hear any shots, or anything, really, I want you to run to the bathroom behind the kitchen and climb into the tub. We don't have a full safe room in this place, but I did have them reinforce the walls and door of that bathroom in particular."

Her eyes looked huge in her face, but she nodded her understanding.

"If you give me a gun, I can back you up." He couldn't have been more shocked if a kitten had offered to cover him, but then he realized that she was the daughter and sister of soldiers. She might be a better shot than he was. *Merde*, she was magnificent.

He shook his head regretfully. "I only have one tucked away in each room. I'll be back as soon as I can, *bébé*." He spoke as he was walking, not wanting to waste time, but turned just before leaving the room. "It's really probably nothing...just more storm damage." He wished he felt as certain of that as he sounded.

Marina heard the underlying message behind his words. The noise was likely weather-related, but he was rattled, too. Something felt strange to her...but maybe it was just disconcerting to be stranded in a blizzard in Vermont with no power. She took three deep, cleansing breaths, willing her heart to slow down, and was relieved when at least there were no shots immediately. That had to be a good sign.

Of course, it could also mean that Pierre had been surprised and was lying upstairs in a puddle of his own blood, wishing she'd come to help him. Or, no, that wasn't his style. If he were hurt, he'd be relieved that at least he'd managed to spare her. He was ultra-protective, and she actually really like that about him, but she had also grown used to taking care of herself over the years. As another minute ticked by, again feeling like a lifetime, she decided that she was through with sitting on the sidelines. She squared her shoulders and raised her chin, about to take a step to follow him, when Pierre returned, moving so silently that she was impressed by his skill, in spite of what must still be painful injuries.

The picture he made, the tall, handsome man with a grim face set in stone, dressed all in black with tousled hair and holding a gun as if he'd been born with it in his hand, was so different from everything she'd ever thought—every image she'd ever seen of him in a magazine or online—that it was laughable. Frankly, she liked this Pierre better—a whole hell of a lot better. In response to her questioning look, he gave a quick shake of his head.

"It was the window in your bedroom. It appears as if a large tree was blown, shattering the window in and setting off the alarm. I checked the room over, but there's glass everywhere, so it's hard to tell. I'd like to look outside, too, but frankly, it's gotten too dark to see much, if anything."

Marina digested his words. "What would you be looking for outside?"

Pierre flicked the safety back onto the gun and walked carefully back over to the hidden compartment in the couch where he kept the fingerprint-coded lockbox he'd pulled it out of, then bent to replace it. He cleared his throat and his expression darkened before he answered.

"Not sure…and I could be way off, but I don't like this number of coincidences. We're in the middle of a storm and that would be the most obvious explanation, but—"

He paused and she finished his thought. "But something feels weird."

Pierre's nod was clipped. "I hope you'll forgive me if I have become a bit, ah, paranoid after recent events."

Marina managed a credible smile. "Sure, as long as you forgive me, too," she returned.

His voice lowered. "There is absolutely nothing to forgive you for, *chérie*. You're… I'm not even sure how to describe you. Brave, kind, sexy…special." He broke off uncomfortably and did a slow lap around the room, not looking at her.

Marina felt her cheeks heat, taken completely by surprise at the underlying note of honesty in his unexpected praise.

When he finished his circuit, she felt compelled to answer.

"I'm not, you know. I'm not really brave or sexy…and probably not as special as the women you're used to."

He stared at her for a long moment, his dark eyes almost black in the light that was dimmer from the fire that had died down, and his expression was nearly inscrutable, but something in his gaze was tender. "Why don't you let me be the judge of that, hm?"

The flare of heat that rose in her belly had nothing to do with the fire or embarrassment, but pure, unbridled lust. She walked quickly toward the doorway.

"I'll, uh, get ready for bed, then," she said in a rush.

Pierre's voice, when it came, was much closer than she expected. Damn, the man moved like a freaking cat.

No, not even like a housecat but like a panther – silent, swift and deadly.

"It's not safe for you to go to your room, with all the glass, and I reset the alarms so any movement of any door will make them go off again," he cautioned. "Also, I don't think we should split up, if we can help it. Even if not for safety reasons, then to stay warm," he added.

"Right," Marina replied, rubbing her arms unconsciously as she realized how cold the room had become without her noticing. "I remember you saying something about that before, um, when the power went out. But...we'll sleep here? Together?" She hated the breathy note in her voice, and hoped that none of the totally inappropriate excitement she felt at the idea came across to Pierre.

His chuckle was rich and amused. "It's an enormous couch, *bébé*. I think we can manage to squeeze onto it together." He teased her, and her inner channel clenched at his choice of words. "Plus, it's near the fire," he added in more pragmatic tone. "Why don't I build the flames up again while you go... What's that quaint expression one of our other nannies taught us? Go powder your nose? The bathroom's right over there, and we have a woodpile reserve room right off the living room, too, so everything's connected and shouldn't set off any alarms."

Marina agreed hastily, eager to get away from him for a moment, and grabbed the giant flashlight again to make the trip. Alone in the bathroom, a tastefully-decorated oasis that felt a little bit like stepping into a winter woodland paradise in a five-star hotel, she took stock of herself, physically and emotionally. She was drained...and, she ruefully acknowledged to her reflection in the mirror, made somewhat eerie-looking by the small artificial light source, she looked it. Her hair was a tangled mass, her face was dirty, and while her injuries had improved, the adrenaline and painkillers were wearing off, so she was sore. She definitely didn't feel special. Still, the fact that Pierre thought so warmed her in every way, and she hugged his words to herself, even as she began to shake slightly from the cold the longer she spent away from the Great Room.

She opened the medicine cabinet and was happy to find several new toothbrushes and tubes of toothpaste, still in their wrappers, although really it was unsurprising, considering that this was a Gaspard family residence, albeit a small one. They probably kept every single bathroom stocked with such niceties in all their houses. Brushing her teeth made her feel a little more restored and gave her the impetus to take the plunge and scrub her hands with the icy water, and even splash some water on her face, though it made her gasp and tremble harder. When her fingers started feeling numb, she turned off the silver tap and dried her face quickly before hurrying back out into the living room, which promised instant heat.

She made a beeline for the couch and, feeling shivery and suddenly even more exhausted than she'd been, she jumped into the nest of blankets that they'd left when they'd gotten up so abruptly before. She could see Pierre's distinct form, so tall and proud, both strong and elegant, as he shifted firewood, and the sight comforted her at the same as it made her shudder in a good way, awakening every nerve in her body. Much as she wanted to keep enjoying the view, soon the warmth of the fire and the blankets, combined with her utter exhaustion, had her fighting to keep her eyelids open and she lost the battle.

Pierre thought he'd been quick, and he'd tried to hurry even more when, out of the corner of his eye, he'd seen Marina streak through the living room like she was frozen, but he would never again move as fast as he had before his attack. While he'd been able to ignore his knee when he'd rushed upstairs, and he didn't think he'd done permanent damage, the joint had started to scream in protest as he piled more wood onto the fire, building it up as much as he safely could.

It had been a struggle to get all the wood reorganized into an easier configuration from the neat, covered reserve woodpile, since they'd already burned more than he usually would over the course of a week. The chore brought back a rare memory of his dad from before his mom had gotten sick. His father had made more time for his children then, and he'd painstakingly taught his oldest son that even though they could afford to pay anyone to do almost anything for them, it was important that they learn how to be self-sufficient, because a man never knew when he would need to rely on himself — or someone else would rely on him.

When Pierre had limped back into the living room, Marina was curled up under two blankets, deeply asleep. He might have been uncertain, since he couldn't see her face very clearly, but the faint snores that came from her left no doubt. Could a woman's snore be sexy — or was he just so fucking turned on by everything that she did that any sound she made would have made him harder? Even in spite of his injuries and unease about all of the accidents they'd had at the cabin, he could have drilled through a wall with his cock, he was so hot for her. He smiled at the memory of how she'd blushed when he'd mentioned sleeping together on the couch.

He knew he should be a gentleman and sleep on the other side of the sectional. *Putain*, she was asleep. He would not presume that she was okay with him next to her, even if it damn near killed him to put any space between them. When he sat down on the opposite side of the sprawling sofa and tried to find a comfortable position, grabbing another throw blanket, he heard a small mewling sound from the pile of her blankets and went to her immediately, gingerly kneeling down in front of her, careful to favor his bad leg. She was shivering, and when he reached out his hand to touch hers, it was like an ice cube in spite of the fuzzy coverings.

"Still cold, *bébé*?" he asked, torn between anxiety for her and wanting to just let her rest.

Her thick eyelashes fluttered as she mostly opened her eyes, but he wasn't certain if she really saw him.

"So…cold," she confirmed in a voice that was barely more than a whisper. "Water was…so cold."

Pierre cursed himself for not expecting this. It was decently warm by the fire—a hell of a lot warmer than it had been outside—but since the generator had died and they'd let a lot of warmth out of the door, with an upstairs window open, too, the temperature had really dropped in the house. It wasn't freezing, but with the cold, combined with the stress from her accident the day before, the extended time outside and pure anxiety over the alarm, he should have warned her to just use a washcloth, as he had. He wasn't certain if she was fully hypothermic, but he needed to warm her up or she might head in that direction. On a long-ago skiing trip in college, he'd seen it happen very quickly for one of his fellow adventure-seeking friends.

It was no longer a question of acting like a gentleman, and he hated that part of him cheered at the circumstance. He wondered if maybe he really was the bastard so many people called him, but shook away the thought to examine later. Even though Marina might think he was a dick in the morning—something he was generally really used to people thinking, but which made him feel oddly hollow to expect to get from her— this was now a question of safety. He needed to share his body heat. He grabbed the additional blanket then tore off his sweater and t-shirt, throwing them on the floor in a careless pile that normally would have horrified his ultra-organized sensibilities. *Merde*, the air in the living room was cold on his bare chest, and his nipples hardened painfully before he pulled off his trousers as well and nearly dove into the pile of blankets next to Marina in only his thin boxer-briefs.

She curled into him immediately and the feeling of her soft curves pressed into the hard length of his body, even through her clothing, was just as exquisite as he'd dreamed it would be since the first instant he'd seen her. No, he'd dreamed of feeling her this way since the first time he'd seen a picture of her. He didn't allow himself to savor the sensation, though, but instead wrapped his arms around her torso, pulling her as close as he could. After a moment, her shaking slowed considerably, but she still felt cold. Cursing himself for a cad and bastard, he stroked her cheek with one finger.

"*Marinette*, you're still really chilly. I think you should take off your shirt and, uh, pants."

Because of how they were lying, he couldn't see her face clearly, but he felt her lips curve against his chest and guessed she was smiling. Her reply, when it came, was muffled and sultry, which he thought was likely unintentional as she sounded half-awake.

"Know I must be dreaming... Real Pierre has never said anything like that. Thinks I'm off-limits." Just like that, all the blood rushed back to his cock and he hardened again to the point of pain, nestled right up against where her thighs met. But she wasn't done.

"Also...not wearing anything underneath my clothes. Don't wanna get colder," she continued in sleepy protest, and his hands felt like they might be shaking with the effort of not reaching up under her sweater and palming her full breasts.

He exerted the full force of his famous — or infamous — iron will and ignored all the demands of his body. As he'd suspected, she was obviously still uncomfortable from the cold. He could fix that with more skin-to-skin contact. That was all it needed to be, until he could properly seduce her. *Putain de merde*, he *ached* to seduce her.

"This will warm you up, *bébé*. Let me do this for you." Without meaning to, he poured the force of his determination into the words, making them almost a command, albeit a tender one.

"Mmm," she hummed against his chest, her breath tickling the thick, dark hairs there. "Say it like that and I'll do anything."

Every muscle of his body tightened and his cock twitched against her at her words...and the revelation that she really might be into what he needed. Damn, he'd had a feeling. With a Herculean effort, he calmed his body down and tugged at her sweater until she shifted her arms so he could pull it up over her head. The feel of how chilled her skin still was as the diamond-hard points of her nipples rubbed against his chest was enough—barely—to refocus him. He curled down into the blankets to reach her thin trousers, too, and under the covers, the unique, sweet musk of her body surrounded him. He inhaled deeply, his mouth watering to taste the nirvana of her pussy, but he ignored the urge and instead gently worked her pants down her cold legs. As soon as she was free, he straightened up again and curved his larger body around her, entwining their legs and wrapping her in his arms again, trying to get as much skin-to-skin contact as possible.

She stayed cool for another few minutes, but at last, with a sigh of pure contentment, her body relaxed against his, obviously far more comfortable than she'd been before, and the little snuffly snore that he found utterly adorable started up again. Their bodies were so close that every deep, sleeping breath rubbed her ample breasts against him, and he could actually feel the slight moisture of her core against the material of his boxer briefs. If he hadn't kept them on, he would have been hard-pressed not to at least rub himself against her. Even with that thin barrier, he held himself nearly rigidly still, not wanting to inflame his nerves past the breaking point. If women were a drug, he might have just found his opium...the stuff of pure dreams and fantasies. It was a long, long while before he finally drifted off uncomfortably, cock granite-hard and his hands cramped from stopping himself from touching her silky skin.

Chapter Eleven

Marina slowly returned to consciousness on a warm, vibrating mattress. It felt soft to the touch, but was firm and smelled so enticing that she inhaled deeply over and over, rubbing her cheek against something soft. As she cracked her eyes open, she realized that more than half of her nude body was draped on top of a nearly-naked Pierre on the couch, underneath a massive stack of blankets that surrounded them like a giant cocoon. Her cheek rested on the soft mat of dark hair on his chiseled chest, her hand was on his right nipple and one of her legs was thrown over both of his, with something long and hard pressed against her thigh through thin fabric.

She felt amazing—warm in spite of the cold air she could feel on the top of her head where it peeked above the covers—and in the limbo between sleep and wakefulness, she didn't think she'd been more aroused. Ever. Her core was molten and liquid against his hip, and her nipples were hard and aching where they touched his hot skin. She'd had a few dreams about Pierre after their initial encounter — which had surprised and mortified her at the time, since he obviously detested her — but in her dreams, he'd ordered her to come sit on his lap, or kneel in front of him, and something about his voice or the way he commanded her had just driven her right over the edge. She'd woken up panting and reaching for the vibrator that she had gotten years earlier when she and Annelise had daringly visited a sex shop to get decorations for the bachelorette party of a mutual friend.

This dream — and it must be a dream, because she never slept naked — was *way* better than the others, though. When she began to stroke Pierre's chest, his grumble of approval sounded so real. And it truly felt like he shifted next to her so that his cock rubbed against her needy core, so wet that it was practically dripping on him. She kissed his neck and chest, everywhere she could reach, and his large, rough hands roamed over her back and down her sides, settling onto her breasts, which she jutted toward him in silent demand for him to touch them.

She was so into the dream that it took a second for a voice to register — Pierre's voice. She thought maybe he'd said the words twice. Well, *growled* them, really.

"If you're half-asleep and you want to stop, *bébé*, you'd better say it now, because I don't think I'll be able to in another minute."

The truth of their situation returned to her like a jolt of electricity, and she froze. They were snowed in and stranded together. She was with the man-candy of her dreams, who was also an ass, but not as much of an ass as she'd thought — with no power, no generator, and a broken upstairs window. She drew her eyebrows together.

"Um, I think I was mostly still asleep...catching up now, but I don't remember why I'm naked."

She felt his deep, rusty chuckle as well as heard it close to her ear, and it made something loosen and melt inside her chest. This man kept his kindness well-hidden, but it was there all the same, more than maybe even he was aware of.

"You wake up with a near-stranger touching you, a hairs-breadth away from sinking into your pussy, and the only thing you ask is why you're naked? *Ma Marinette*, you're incredible...wonderful."

"You're not really a stranger anymore, I think, Pierre...and I was touching you, too. I think any other man would be inside me right now."

He groaned and the sound was filled with true agony. "You're killing me, *chérie. Killing* me. And you have no idea." He took a shaky breath, closing his eyes. "You're naked because you were freezing last night. I just built up the fire again a little while ago, but yesterday I had to warm you up with my body, too."

Marina had a fuzzy recollection of shivering under the blankets, then having a wild conversation and Pierre taking off her clothes. "I thought that was just another dream, too," she blurted without thinking.

"You've been dreaming of me, have you?" Pierre's voice was like gravel, and it made her tingle all over again.

She thought of lying, but what was the point? If they had only this, why not be as honest as they had been last night?

"Yes," she whispered. "All the time since that night at the Mount Valder. I wanted to think you were an asshole—I *did* think that—but I finally decided that I must be really attracted to assholes."

The sound that Pierre made was almost like a strangled whimper, and his face looked pained. "*Merde, bébé*, you have no idea what it does to me to hear you say that. But I have to tell you that I might be a good brother, and maybe a good boss, but I *am* an asshole—a royal prick in bed, especially. I crave…certain things."

Marina guessed that he expected her to run away screaming at the idea that he might be kinky, but instead she was intrigued.

"What do you need? Is it something you're afraid I won't be able to give you?"

He tipped his head back as far as their position would allow and grunted, the sound making her quiver inside.

"Control. Dominance. And I'm afraid you *will* be able to give it to me. You might truly enjoy letting me control you when I want to…*need* to…but challenge me in every other way." He opened his eyes and stared at her, his gaze deep and searching. "Like no other, *Marinette*."

Like lightning, everything from the past two days and the few months since they'd met at the soiree at the fancy Boston social club came back to her in a rush of understanding so stark and clear it was almost painful. She was always playing things safe because she hadn't ever really been tempted to take a chance. Annelise was right. It was relatively easy to remain faithful to Jaime's memory because she had grieved deeply, yes, but also because she had never truly been moved by anyone. There was a part of her that just hadn't been touched — a part she'd thought *couldn't* be touched by anyone else.

But everything about Pierre, even that first night when she'd been so mortified and angry, had attracted her in spite of herself. Now that she knew more about him, why he was the way he was, now that she had begun to really care for him, she could see that she was also wildly attracted to him. To that part of him, too.

She thrilled at the idea of him controlling her, yearned for it. Even hearing him speak it out loud made her hotter than she'd ever felt, every nerve ending sparking, ready. The idea of not ever experiencing the passion he offered, of not seizing the chance to feel like a whole woman, complete with sexual desires and needs being fulfilled by the man of her dreams, was unthinkable. She'd been skirting around the idea in her mind, but in that moment, she made her decision.

"I want to give myself to you, Pierre. To be yours."

This time, the sound he made was unmistakably a growl. In a hurricane of blankets, he pounced on her, slanting his lips over hers in a soulful kiss that felt like it lit her body on fire.

Pierre could barely believe what Marina was telling him. In fact, he felt nearly numb with shock, mixed with burgeoning hope, as he watched her lips moving. But her eyes...her *eyes*...were what convinced him. In their depths, he read real arousal and affection—and deep need. As soon as he recognized that, she was his. *His*.

He kissed her fiercely, then tenderly, sucking and nibbling at the soft fullness of her lips before stroking into her mouth with his tongue when she gasped in pleasure. He covered her with his body, pressing her into the soft cushions and stroking up and down the velvety skin of her arms and along her sides with his fingertips. She felt soft and curvy underneath him on the pillowy couch, and he luxuriated in the feel of her, the contrasts between them. At his touch, she squirmed and pushed her hips helplessly against his swollen cock in a steady rhythm until he could feel the moisture of her arousal seeping through the thin fabric of his boxer-briefs.

She was like wildfire, running her hands and nails up along the muscles of his back and opening her thighs to cradle him, wrapping her long, lean legs around him and crossing her ankles behind his lower back. She mewled with pleasure, throwing back her head, as he kissed down her hot cheek to her neck, inhaling the indescribable fruity, spicy scent of her hair, like peaches and vanilla mixed with woodsmoke. When he bit the soft flesh right where her neck met her shoulder, she cried out and shivered, tightening her arms and legs, and her nails dug into his back so hard that they gave him goosebumps. He thought his cock might just burst before he could even feel the paradise of her pussy.

"You like that, hm?" he rumbled into her ear, and she gave a breathless groan of assent. "*Tell me,*" he prompted, and pulled away slightly so he could look at her face. Her eyes were glazed with passion, and her lips were swollen from their kisses. She looked rumpled, messy and delicious.

"Yes…*Dios, yes,* I love it," she breathed.

"That's what I wanted to hear, *bébé.* Tell me when you like something. I want to learn every inch of your beautiful body until you're screaming with pleasure for your man." He punctuated his statement by raising himself slightly to make a little space between their bodies, careful to keep the warm covers mostly over them, sliding his hands up to feather light caresses over the swollen peaks of her nipples. She nearly convulsed in response...*so sensitive*, his woman.

"Pierre...the way you talk, the way you touch me... You're driving me *crazy*." Her voice was a husky whisper, and he wasn't sure she even realized what she was saying, she seemed so deeply immersed in the sensations.

"Spread your legs and let me drive you totally insane, *ma Marinette*, before I embarrass myself for the first time with a woman."

She tensed, just for an instant, then it felt like she deliberately relaxed. He was confused. Then he cursed himself for being so blind, especially after her confession the night before. She obviously wasn't very experienced, but was it possible he could be her first? The thought was as sobering as it was exhilarating, and he had to stifle the primal urge to mark her, claim her, immediately.

He managed to drag his better nature to the forefront. "I'm... This isn't your first time, is it, *chérie*?"

She blushed and bit her lower lip. "No..." she started a little haltingly. "But, uh, you'll be the second. And the first was...nothing to write home about. My fault, I think, not his."

He hadn't thought that his cock could possibly grow any larger or harder, but incredibly, at her words, he actually felt it swell as if it strained toward her, like some sort of homing beacon. His mind was equally engaged, realizing that she was nearly untouched, which made her eagerness even more enticing. *Damned near irresistible.*

"God, *bébé*...it was *not* your fault, and he was obviously a fool, but I think I could kiss him for his stupidity since it allowed me to find you."

145

Her surprised laughter was sexy as hell, but it cut off with a gasp as the movement of her chest made her nipples brush against his hands, still cupped loosely over them.

"No kissing other people," she scolded breathlessly, and he thrilled at the possessive note in her voice. Odd, because any hint of possessiveness or deep attachment from any woman in his past had made him run for the hills, but as with everything else, Marina was different.

"Agreed on one condition," he answered, and his voice grew raspy with lust. "Let me lap up all that sweet honey you've been making, right from the source."

Her breath hitched, so he knew his words had aroused her, but she hesitated.

"What is it?" he rumbled.

"Do you...really want to? I know some guys don't, um, like it."

Bon Dieu, she was adorable and she had no idea how sexy she was. He reached his hand down between them to stroke his finger, oh so lightly into her wetness, making her gasp and quickly coating the digit. He held her gaze as he brought it back up to his mouth and slowly sucked it in, licking her salty-sweet juices with relish.

"Any man worth taking inside your body, *chérie*, cares about his partner's pleasure as much as his own," he rasped, and meant it. "Are you going to open up for me?"

She let her thighs fall open with a sigh and he knew that his smile of satisfaction was probably feral, but he didn't care. He would make this incredible for her.

Marina had thought it would be hard to find anything sexier than Pierre's words and the fervent appreciation behind them, especially when she'd always felt so uncomfortable with the idea of a man putting his mouth on that part of her, but at the first drawn-out laps of his tongue along her slit, she realized how terribly wrong she'd been. It felt amazing…so amazing that she nearly arched right off the couch as she went stiff. Pierre chuckled, a dark, vibrating chuckle right against her pussy that sent delicious sparks everywhere throughout her body, then clamped his hands around her thighs to hold her in place.

"Glad you liked that, *chérie*, but I can't have you bumping your head. Hold still and let me fuck you with my mouth."

She panted her response. She wasn't sure what she'd said, but it must have satisfied him because he bent his dark head again between her legs and drove her to the very brink of insanity. He traced the tip of his tongue around her bundle of nerves with exquisite gentleness, then sucked and licked up and down the length of her, lingering when something felt extra sexy until she thought she might not be able to take it anymore. She'd made herself come before, even figured at one point that any orgasm a man could give her was probably about the same as the ones she gave herself, but as she built toward an elusive, shimmering *something* now, it was nothing like she'd ever felt before. When he stroked into her with one long, thick finger, curling it inside her, her pleasure overcame her like a freight train of electric sensation, knocking her over and firing every nerve at once until all she could feel was bliss, floating nearly outside of her body.

The pleasure went on and on, and she gave herself over to it, helpless as she tugged on Pierre's thick hair, not sure whether she was tugging him away or pulling him even closer. When she finally came back to herself a little, he was still lapping at her, and she shivered with another round of delicious aftershocks.

"I like the way you scream, *bébé*."

"Oh my God, Pierre... That was unbelievable. I don't...never even imagined..." She felt like an idiot, but she couldn't describe how he'd made her feel.

Pierre licked his lips, still glistening with her honey, and raised one dark, amused eyebrow, half-sitting up. "Hm, I think you might be even sexier when you're fucked speechless."

Instead of trying to continue to put words together, she turned so she was on the edge of the couch and dropped down to her knees in front of him, keeping one blanket wrapped around her back, feeling a thrill of womanly power at the undeniable flare of lust in his dark gaze. Her leg gave a little twinge of protest but felt mostly healed.

"Let me show you, then," she said.

At her throaty words, Pierre tensed all over and his face became a mask of desire.

An instant earlier, she would have said that she was too wrung out to feel even a spark of arousal for at least a few minutes, but watching his eyes go heavy-lidded and seeing his fists clench helplessly, all because she'd knelt before him, just as she had in her dreams, made her desire flood back in a rush like hot lava.

"*Mon Dieu, chérie*, to see you like this... You're so fucking sexy. I want to, but if you put your mouth on me, I might go off like a rocket." He rubbed the thick bulge of his cock as he spoke, and she heard unvarnished honesty in his voice. "I need to be inside you — need that so goddamn badly, to feel your pretty cunt all around me, milking me. Let me get a condom."

When he would have risen, she put a hand on his thigh.

"I'm on birth control, and I'm clean," she said, her voice a little shy, when she was talking to someone who'd had his mouth on her not five minutes earlier.

Pierre's whole body tensed so hard that every muscle went taut, and even his jaw twitched. "Ah, *merde*, I was so determined to be a better man for you, but then you say that and I don't think I can be." He stroked her cheek, and something in his expression made her thrill. "I promise I have been tested since my last lover, months ago, and I'm clean too, so if you're sure, I would like nothing more than to feel your sweet pussy."

She straightened up on her knees, rubbing her nipples along the wiry hairs on his thighs as she went, and hooked her fingers into the waistband of his shorts.

"I'm sure," she confirmed, starting to pull them down. "And I like you just the way you are." She finished, pulling them off to reveal the monster erection that rose, enormous and thick, straight up from his lap. Partly to reinforce her point, and partly because she couldn't resist the temptation, she licked the single drop of silky pre-cum that had leaked from the tip.

Like a large, waiting predator springing into action all at once, Pierre jumped up and took his shorts off the rest of the way at warp speed. He kissed her, a deep, searching kiss, so that she tasted herself on his lips, then sank back down on couch. Even though the position put him lower than her, she felt as if he were still dominating her, looming over her, just by the way he held her gaze.

"Come over here and sit on my lap, *bébé*. Those gorgeous nipples are begging to be sucked. Keep your blanket just like that so you don't get cold."

There was a gush of moisture in her core at the tone of his sexy command and as soon as she was close enough, he pulled her onto his lap so that his cock was trapped, nestled between the lips of her pussy.

He bent his head to her chest and took one sensitive nipple into the warm cavern of his mouth, reaching up with one hand to gently pinch the other. She threw her head back and realized with a strangled moan that in this position, any movement by her rubbed his length right against her clit. Pierre sucked her nipple harder, tracing around it with his tongue before sucking it back in, driving her wild as she bucked helplessly against him. When he finally released her nipple with an audible pop, she thought her heart might just thump right out of her chest from the onslaught of pleasure. When she tried to rise up over his lap, though, he stopped her with two strong hands on her shoulders.

"Not yet, *bébé*. Don't want the other one to get jealous," he teased, and she screamed as he pulled the nipple he'd been pinching into his mouth. Just when she thought she might come from the way he was playing with her breasts, he released her other nipple, too, and lifted her with two hard hands under her butt right onto his cock.

He was so strong that he was able to lower her, inch by devastating inch, onto his length until he was fully seated. The pressure of his entrance was a little uncomfortable — it had been so long and the one other man she'd been with had definitely been smaller — but her extreme arousal meant that she was practically dripping, and he slid in all the way without any issue.

"Ok, *chérie*?" he asked carefully, even as his neck was tensed from arousal, and she felt a wave of tenderness for this man who hid his kindness deep under a gruff, harsh shell.

"God, yes," she breathed. She clenched around him and felt incredibly full, connected in a way she couldn't have imagined.

"*Dieu merci*," he grunted, and she only had a second to be amused as he bucked upward from underneath, making her gasp at the sensation and also causing her breasts to bobble in his face. His smile was predatory, a bright slash of white in the dim room. "You feel like paradise, *Marinette*, and the view is fucking glorious."

She wanted to laugh, but he moved again and her breath caught in her throat. She put her arms up onto his shoulders to steady herself, and couldn't help but trace the planes of his muscles with tenderness for an instant before he thrust again. Then, she held on for dear life as she was overcome with the electric pleasure of him filling her, over and over.

"So deep," she moaned. "So good." She struggled to form any sort of coherent speech, trying to give him the words he wanted. His expression was intense, carved from granite, but she could see how her encouragement fanned the flames of his desire, and he thrust faster, but still kept a steady rhythm that was driving her to the brink of madness.

The slapping sound of her going up and down on his lap was muffled by the blankets that were still mostly all around them, but where they slipped off and her skin was exposed, goosebumps rose from the cold. Instead of making her uncomfortable, it only added to the sensation, and she bucked her hips as much as his hands would allow, trying to take more of him, deeper, faster. The smell of the wood-burning fire mixed with the spicy, rich scent of Pierre's skin until she felt almost drunk.

"Please," she begged, not really sure what she was begging for, only that she needed it so badly. "Pierre, *please*."

At the sound of his name on her lips, Pierre's eyes went even darker, and he felt wilder as he bucked in a frenzy below her for a moment before he held himself still, obviously bringing himself under control.

"Run over to the fireplace, *bébé*. It will be cold, but I want to see you next to the *loup-garou*." His voice was almost inhumanly deep, a raspy, guttural command. It made her shiver and she clenched all around him. She nodded, mesmerized by his predator's gaze.

She was so wet that it made a squelching sound as she rose off him, and the feeling of his cock dragging against her every nerve, along with the shocking cold when she threw the blanket off, made her suck in a sharp, surprised breath. She held his gaze for a long moment, willing him to understand that she was doing this for him, would have done almost anything for him in that moment, to please him and please herself, before she hurried over to the enormous hearth.

He'd told her he'd built up the fire again, but the flames blazed even higher and hotter than she'd expected, nearly filling the massive fireplace. The air, uncomfortably chilly near the couch, grew much warmer almost instantly, and when her feet touched the stones nearest one of the werewolf statues, she felt almost toasty.

As she looked back over her shoulder, Pierre resembled a pagan king, surrounded by fuzzy blankets that looked like furs in the firelight, unabashedly naked. He sat with his legs spread and his erection rising large and proud in front of him, glistening with the moisture from her arousal. His muscles were tense and chiseled, but his lips were soft. His eyes held warm appreciation and approval. It was clear that he loved watching her, and a warm shiver coursed through her body at how much she enjoyed being watched.

"So beautiful, *bébé*, waiting for your man to come fill you again." His deep voice filled the space, even though he didn't speak loudly. Her nipples tightened even more at his words, and she held his gaze from across the room.

"Pierre, *please*," she urged again.

When he smiled, a grin of dark amusement and sensual promises, goosebumps rose again—not from cold but from arousal.

"Careful, *chérie*. You could get me to do just about anything when you use that voice. Pierre, please what?" He reached down one hand to stroke the thickness of his cock almost lazily, but his breathing sped up.

"Please…come here," she finished, and another thrill coursed through her when he rose and crossed the room to stand so close that she could feel his body heat, but not touching her.

"What would you like me to do, *Marinette*? I want to hear you ask me." His voice was commanding, but strained with desire. This close to the fire, the flames blazed like molten lava, covering the brown of his dark eyes entirely with red.

"I want you to…" She bit her lip, blushing again. "Put yourself in me," she finished in a rush.

He took the last step until his skin brushed against hers, and reached down, sinking two thick fingers into her with a wet sound. She moaned and pushed her butt back toward him.

"Is that what you wanted, *bébé*?" he teased, reaching his other hand to tweak her nipple, still sensitive from his earlier treatment and making her gasp.

"I love it," she whispered. "But I need…more." She wiggled her butt, reveling in how good he felt, but longing for him to fill her again.

"Say the words and it's yours, whatever you want," he urged in a dark, rumbling voice so low it was nearly a whisper. She could tell he was not as unaffected as he pretended.

He increased the pace of the movement of his fingers inside her channel and moved his other hand to her other breast. Marina tried to work up the courage to say the words—which seemed ridiculous, since he'd already been inside her, but certain modesties were incredibly difficult to overcome—but the overwhelming sensations soon left no room for any other thought but how amazing he felt, and how much more amazing the hard length of him, so stiff and swollen as it brushed her hip, would feel. When he pulled his fingers out of her, it left an acute emptiness that made her ache.

"Pierre…" she stammered, nervous but determined to finish. "I want you to fuck me with your huge cock. Fill me—" She didn't know what else she might have said, because he thrust into her with one long stroke and her mind just went haywire.

The sensation of him filling her again, from behind, with the heat of the fire in front of her and the blazing warmth of him behind her, was indescribable. It felt like he touched every nerve along the walls of her pussy, then bumped up against something deep inside that had never been touched before. For one shimmering instant, she felt as if they became one, joined together in something beyond the physical or even emotional. She reveled in his fullness, the deep grunting sound he made. When she looked back over her shoulder at his face, what she saw there made her heart and her pussy clench. He looked savage, but also tender. She put out one hand to brace herself and touched the smooth stone of the carved werewolf that he had created so long ago. A monster on the outside, hard and tough, but the eyes showed the werewolf as a man, complete with flaws and vulnerabilities.

She screamed with each long stroke, her pleasure building again, so fast that it was almost painful. When he shifted his hips slightly to push into her more deeply, the change sent her hurtling over the precipice into pure, undiluted ecstasy. A hoarse cry tore out of her throat and clenched every muscle at once as electric whirls of pleasure washed over her like waves. Behind her, Pierre thrust into her several more times, making her scream again, until with a bellow he began to fill her with pulse after pulse of hot cream. Her pussy convulsed and undulated all around him, and the grip that he had on her hips, holding her tight against his cock, felt like it might leave bruises. He was all that held her up as he emptied himself inside her, every spurt of seed setting off another delicious quake.

She wasn't sure how, since it felt like the world went fuzzy in a combination of Pierre's impossibly handsome, arrogant face that made her melt with affection, along with the monstrous but lonely face of the *loup-garou*, but somehow Pierre got them back to the couch, limbs entwined under a pile of blankets. As she came back to herself fully, he was stroking her hair and her back with the kind of deep tenderness that she never could have imagined him capable of only days earlier.

"You're crying, *bébé*," he said, sounding alarmed.

Chapter Twelve

Fils de putain, Pierre realized he was truly the arrogant asshole everyone called him. He'd been too rough and broken something inside of Marina. Sweet, sassy, brave and sexy-as-hell Marina. Too late, he realized that what he'd secretly always feared was that if he let the dominating beast inside of him loose on someone he might actually care about, he could destroy her. Obviously, he'd been right. Even worse, he'd known she had been injured — albeit relatively minor injuries — but still, he'd pounced on her like the werewolves of legend he'd loved so much when he was younger, before he'd forced himself to become the controlled head of the Gaspard family and company.

"Where did I hurt you, *chérie*? What can I do to make it better?" he asked, feeling helpless. He'd never liked to see women cry — had never known quite what to do. All their emotions were so illogical that he had trouble figuring out where to start unraveling them. For some reason, his question only made her cry harder.

He'd seen some women cry beautifully. His sister was one of them, so elegant when she cried that even when she'd been a little girl, it had seemed almost unnatural. Marina was *not* one of those women. Her eyes puffed up and red streaks appeared on her cheeks.

She did manage to gasp one word, though, that felt like a dagger plunged into his gut and twisted. Hard.

"Jaime."

He reared back as if she'd slapped him, and when she looked up, her expression was heart-breaking. She looked guilty, and apologetic—filled with regret. The amazing experience they'd just shared, that had tilted his very-controlled world on its axis, had made her feel regret. A cold fury, as illogical as it was intense, began to rise inside him but was halted by the blaring of the alarms.

He leaped to his feet, barely feeling the pain of his injured muscles that he really shouldn't have pushed so hard with Marina. Unconsciously, he covered her with the blankets, but didn't bother to wrap one around himself. It would just slow him down. With the same quick, practiced motion he'd used the night before, he got out the gun and stood, rigid, prepared to face the intruder. An unusual sensation—which he realized uncomfortably might be fear, not for himself, but for Marina—made his fingers tingle and his chest ache. He tamped it down ruthlessly, clearing his mind as he'd learned to do when faced with danger, but it was much more difficult than it typically was.

The intruder, when he appeared, was about the last person he would have expected. Marc Constantin, who they described as one of the Gaspard family's senior security experts but was really a co-head of security with Villiers, looked nearly as surprised as Pierre felt.

The facial expression of the ex-soldier and U.S. military hero, usually impassive, revealed much more than usual as he took in Pierre's gun and state of undress. Marc's eyes flickered further when he spotted Marina, huddled under the blankets behind Pierre. Pierre widened his stance unconsciously and leveled his gun toward Marc.

The other man held up his hands. "Whoa, there. Good guy here."

Pierre narrowed his eyes, a sudden, irrational suspicion popping into his head. "Why didn't you enter the security code?"

Marc shook his head, although his short-cropped hair didn't move. "I did, but you have it on lockdown mode." Pierre had observed that Marc's Boston accent came out on his dropped r's more when he was tense, although he didn't betray any of the tension on his face. "You must have changed the lockdown code, and I didn't get an alert because your power is out, so it's on manual."

Pierre let out a deep breath. What Marc was saying was reasonable.

"One-two-zero-three-two-zero-zero-seven," he said, disarming the alarms.

"The day after your father passed away," Marc observed, and Pierre was surprised at the depth of the knowledge of his security agent, although he shouldn't have been. Marc was highly trained. Even with all of his resources, Pierre hadn't been able to figure out what, exactly, his training had been.

The sudden silence was nearly as deafening as the alarm.

"How the *hell* did you get here?" Pierre demanded. He might have decided that he still trusted Marc, but he was still pissed—at Marina and in general. The surprise arrival had made him feel out-of-control, something he generally loathed.

"Well, and it's nice to see you too, bossman," Marc drawled. "Happy to explain, but it would be less distracting if your, ah, two pistols weren't pointing at me."

Marina's huff of laughter behind him was a little watery, but unmistakable. He felt slightly abashed, and picked up the pants that lay crumpled where he'd pulled them off the night before. He put away the gun again and slid on the pants nearly in one quick motion, then turned back expectantly toward Marc.

"The storm finally let up early this morning, faster than they feared. Didn't you notice? So, we took one of the choppers as far as we could then, ah, acquired some new snowmobiles. We had to pay quite a bit, so apologies in advance for *that* bill."

He heard something from Marina's direction that sounded suspiciously like, "I *told* you helicopters were a good idea."

"Fine, whatever on the bill," he waved his hand. "Perhaps the better question is why did you go to these lengths to come?"

Marc raised one eyebrow. "Well, when I got an automated accident alert from Marina's car, then couldn't reach you or her, I got concerned. Particularly in light of the other news I texted you about."

"The last message I got from you was something marked urgent, but my reception cut out before it could download. I thought maybe you were warning me that Marina was on her way, too." At Marc's expression, Pierre got a sick feeling in his stomach.

"No…I mean, yes, I sent you that info too. But I was talking about the news that Claude escaped from custody…with a lot of help."

Pierre's insides turned to liquid for a second. "*Putain de merde…non*, I didn't know that." Marina's sharp gasp of breath cut through him as if through a fog.

The strange events of the past few days now took on a much more sinister slant.

"We have to leave. Make sure my family is safe. Marina needs to be safe." Pierre spoke without thinking, and Marc raised an eyebrow at his words.

"Luc, Rémy and Annelise are locked down at the complex in Montreal."

Pierre narrowed his eyes. "And my sister?"

"You can see for yourself in a few minutes. She's riding over with a couple of guys I brought."

Even from behind him, Marina could tell how coldly furious Pierre was. As if Marc's arrival wasn't surprising enough, the news that Claude had escaped and was on the loose somewhere was positively shocking and terrifying.

"You…took my sister away from the safety of our family complex, which we constantly upgrade security on, to fly in a helicopter and take snowmobiles during the tail end of a blizzard in Vermont?" Pierre took a step closer to Marc, and his voice was low and dangerous.

She wasn't sure if she would have been able to stand her ground, but Marc didn't move so much as a muscle.

"Clothilde is a very strong-willed young woman," he answered in a matter-of-fact tone that held just a hint of admiration that she thought he probably wasn't aware of.

"Yes, she is, but we talked about this." Now Pierre's voice was icy, almost scary in how cold it was.

"So go ahead and fire me." She raised her eyebrows at Marc's words, nearly a taunt. Something odd was going on — something beyond what she could see.

Pierre held his ground for a moment longer before he relaxed, visibly but incrementally. "My sister can be remarkably persuasive, but don't think I won't let us, er" — he glanced back toward her as if he'd almost forgotten her presence — "go our separate ways if necessary," he finished.

What an utterly bizarre way of phrasing it, she thought. Marina had finally managed to wiggle into Pierre's sweater from the night before without leaving the blankets, so she stood up and was happy to see that because Pierre was so much taller than her, it fell nearly to her knees. The look Pierre gave her was pure heat, followed quickly by regret — and maybe anger? He cleared his throat.

"You need to make sure Marina and my sister are safe." It was an unmistakable order.

"I think Marc needs to make sure you're safe, too, Pierre," Marina countered. Now, when he looked at her, the cool, aloof mask was firmly back in place. Her heart turned over a little.

"*You* don't need to worry about my safety." It was a dismissal, plain and simple.

She raised her chin and her temper rose. "I think we need to talk about earlier…what happened. I don't think you understood."

Pierre's face was nearly expressionless, but she thought she saw a hint of hurt before arrogance eclipsed it. "This isn't the time, but even if it were, there isn't anything that needs to be said. You need to leave.

We both got what we wanted, especially me, and now I don't want you here."

His words were like a slap, and surprised tears stung her eyes, the same way they would have if he had physically struck her across her cheeks. Marc shuffled uncomfortably but did his best to pretend he wasn't listening.

"You can come with me, Marina," Clothilde said, stepping into the room looking like the cover of a high-fashion snowboarding magazine, if such a thing existed. *In fact, such a thing should exist just so they could ask Clothilde Gaspard to be on the cover.* Marina felt like a wilted mess in her too-large cashmere sweater.

"We can go pack whatever you want while my complete *conard* of a brother, who is *absolument stupide*, talks to his security lackey," Clothilde continued.

Marina wasn't certain, but she was pretty sure that Marc had winced at Clothilde's description, and Pierre looked thunderous that his sister had called him the equivalent of an absolutely stupid jackass.

"Where are the other guys who were supposed to come with you?" Marc asked, his voice businesslike.

"Scouting the perimeter or something equally security-like." Clothilde made the words sound like describing it in more detail was beneath her. Marina had noticed an unusual dynamic between Clothilde and Marc the first few times she'd seen them together, and it had only seemed to become more tense. It was doubly strange today, since it sounded like the younger woman had insisted on coming with Marc. "We can do whatever you'd like, Marina," Clothilde added with genuine kindness.

Part of Marina wanted to stay and insist that Pierre listen to her, but another, larger part quailed at trying to explain how she felt in front of two other people. Still, she would have done it if Pierre had shown the slightest inclination to listen to her explanation. He deserved the truth, instead of whatever he'd imagined, no matter how difficult it was for her.

She opened her mouth to try again, but he forestalled her.

"I am not interested in anything you have to say right now, Ms. Lopez." His tone was cool and faintly condescending, almost exactly the same as it had been that first night at the Mount Valder. Had she just imagined that he'd seemed different? Seen what she'd wanted to see instead of what was really there?

Her vision grew wavy with tears of mortification at the brusque set-down, but she refused to allow them to fall. "You know, I think I will take you up on your kind offer, Clothilde. We can just grab my purse upstairs and I'll put on some more appropriate clothes so we can go."

She was proud of how steady she felt marching up the steps, her back painfully straight.

"Je sais pas qu'est-ce qui se passe, mais je ne t'aime pas trop en ce moment."

His sister's harshly whispered parting words, telling him she didn't know what was happening but that she didn't like him very much right now, still rang in his ears. Pierre wasn't sure he held himself in very high esteem at this point, either, but he'd needed to get Marina to leave. He wanted her safe. That part was true. Obviously, if the accidents at the cabin had been deliberate attacks, as he suspected they were, then she'd been in incredible danger being so close to him. If part of his desperation to get her to leave was also because he didn't want to hear her apologize for how much she still loved her lost, perfect hero, Jaime, then he wasn't going to acknowledge that. He couldn't compete with a dead man, much less a dead first love who had been killed serving his country. A man so principled that he'd denied Marina when she'd thrown herself at him. Pierre had spent one night next to her and would have crawled across broken glass to suck on just one of her beautiful, dusky nipples.

It hurt him in a way he hadn't realized he could still be hurt to realize that when all he could think about was how amazing making love to her had been, she'd been crying—no, *sobbing*—for another man. He didn't need to hear more. He'd deliberately hurt her to get her to leave faster, so she and Clothilde would be safely away from him. He'd tried to get Marc Constantin to leave with them, but the other man had refused.

Pierre had always suspected he'd been the true target of most of the attacks, and he thought his private security guard must agree. It just made more sense that Claude would hate *him* out of all the Gaspards. He was the one who Claude should blame the most if the twisted logic was that by taking over the company, he'd somehow forced Jean-Marie to leave and start his own venture. The truth of it really didn't matter, only what Claude perceived in his own warped thinking.

Trying to erase from his mind the image of Marina's beautiful, expressive face, so incredibly sad and wounded as she'd left with Clothilde and one of the other security guys, he turned back to Marc. They sat at the kitchen table with the remaining security team member who'd just given the report on what they'd found outside. The news was grim.

"How the hell did Claude escape?" he asked Marc, scrubbing his hand over his face and feeling like he'd aged ten years in ten minutes.

Marc looked as pissed off as Pierre felt, and oddly, it made him feel better.

"He had inside and outside help. Someone is funding him, working with him, and they have deep pockets." Marc's lips were a grim line and he drummed his scarred fingers on the table.

"We're talking as deep as mine, right? Or close to it? I mean, that has to narrow the field of potentials. Contacts who can possibly be linked to Claude's other criminal activities who are incredibly wealthy."

Marc let out a frustrated breath. "Yeah, that was our thought, too. But whoever it is, he or she is one slippery bastard. And cruel as hell, too. Every time we get a contact or lead, they disappear, and half the time they turn up dead."

"What do you make of what Clark and... I'm sorry," he turned to the younger security force member. "I'm afraid I've forgotten your name."

"Barnes, sir. Tim Barnes."

Pierre felt ancient, looking at the young man, who couldn't be a day over twenty-one. "You don't have to call me 'sir'. Only this guy." He gestured toward Marc, then turned back to him. "What do you make of what Clark and Barnes found outside?"

Marc considered the question. "It isn't anything obvious, but that tree that you said came down while you were fixing the generator and the tree that hit the generator to begin with? Neither of them should have come down. It's still not great out there, so it isn't absolutely clear if they were cut with something, if someone was careful, but damn, it really looks like he might have been here. Did anything happen inside?"

The hairs rose on the back of Pierre's neck. "Something broke the window in Marina's room. We thought it came from outside, and it set off the alarm, but…your guys should definitely have a look."

Marc nodded almost imperceptibly at Barnes, who jumped to attention and went upstairs without being asked.

"If he was here, we were in more danger than we knew. *Merde*, I left Marina alone to fix the generator. She was a sitting duck." Pierre shook his head, feeling both a sense of delayed horror and crippling relief that she hadn't been hurt more.

"You were both lucky, but you also did the right things. It sounds like she saved your life outside." Marc paused uncomfortably. "I know we're not friends, but why did you — ?"

Pierre cut him off, standing up from his chair with a scrape of wooden chair legs on tile. "You're right. We are not friends," he answered, his tone clipped and forbidding.

They both turned in surprise when Barnes came back down the stairs, an expression of deep concern on his face. It hadn't been more than a minute.

"Sir, I think you need to see this," he said to Marc. The junior team member didn't look as young to Pierre anymore. Now his eyes were the ageless eyes of a warrior. Pierre bolted upstairs, ignoring the twinges in his body, skipping steps and intent on getting to the room where Marina had been staying.

When he skidded to a stop, still only in his stocking feet, the room looked innocuous enough. Well, as innocuous as it could with only a crude barrier put up over the window, just to keep some of the air out. In fact, did the barrier look like it had moved since he'd hurriedly placed it the night before? Something on the bedspread caught his eye. It looked like a picture of three people — small, like something sized for carrying in a wallet. When he stepped closer, he saw that the two women in the picture were familiar. Annelise and Marina. Marina's happy expression, so different from the way she'd looked as she'd left, was like a punch to the gut. He didn't recognize the third person, a man, but his resemblance to Marina was unmistakable. It had to be her brother, Eduardo.

"It was tucked behind the bed, against the wall," Barnes explained.

Pierre was just starting to wonder why something as mundane as a picture that Marina must have somehow dropped had alarmed the younger security agent when he flipped it over.

The room felt like it expanded then contracted as he recognized the handwriting on the back of the photo — so familiar from years of cards and notes — but when he read the words, a loud buzzing seemed to fill the air and he thought he might have swayed on his feet. Marc moved next to him.

'Pretty girl…I love a screamer.'

"Mon Dieu…mon Dieu. He was here. All night." Pierre let the picture flutter back to the bedspread from nerveless fingers, suddenly unable to hold on to it.

He dropped down onto the bed as Marc worked his way around the room, crouching near the window, then again near the closet. Pierre considered the timing, and the dread he'd felt earlier blossomed into full-blown horror. Claude had escaped from custody and could have gone free. Heaven knew he probably had enough money stashed away secretly somewhere to go anywhere, escape permanently and live in comfort in exile. But instead he'd chosen to follow Pierre — or maybe even Marina herself — and use the cover of a blizzard to attack them. It seemed incredible, preposterous. *Unhinged*...like the acts of a madman.

Claude must have come into the house when they'd been outside near the generator. He must have broken the window to the bedroom, but either the extra alarm had surprised him or it was too much of a drop. Then...yes, somehow he must have hidden in the closet, trapped in there unless he wanted to set the alarm off again, until Marc had come in that morning.

"*Merde...merde, merde, merde*," Pierre cursed himself, nearly pulling his hair out of his head from the roots as he ran his hands through it. "I never checked the bedroom closet. I was searching for storm damage, some sort of external threat. I never imagined — "

"How could you know he was inside? It's an absolutely insane stunt. Truly deranged. At least you had the lockdown alarm set, or..." Marc halted and his eyes shuttered.

It was a kindness that Marc trailed off, but Pierre knew what he could have said. If they hadn't set the lockdown alarms that activated every door and window, Claude could have butchered the two of them as they'd slept.

"Fresh footsteps outside, sir...separate from mine and Clark's. Smaller," Barnes reported from the window, and Pierre's sense of wrongness grew.

"Did we get this all wrong, Constantin?" He looked at Marc with dawning horror, noting the same urgent concern reflected in the guy's eyes. In fact, Marc Constantin looked as if he had almost as much invested in the outcome, on a personal level, as Pierre. If the immediate situation weren't so dire, Pierre would have been determined to get to the bottom of that. As it was, he only had one thought. He needed to get to Marina and Clothilde, to ensure that they were safe. He'd made a serious miscalculation, sending them away to protect them.

"Barnes, any word from Clark?" Marc barked.

"Not yet—" The younger man paused as he looked at what appeared to be some sort of large sat phone. "Wait, yes, the roads have been cleared up to the main lodge, and the girls, uh, ladies, decided to leave right away to head for a hotel."

Marc muttered something under his voice that sounded like, "Damn it, Clothilde." Pierre would have chastised him, but he felt like saying the same thing.

"Try to stop him, and we'll head back ASAP." Pierre was halfway out the door, heading to suit- and gear-up to go out in the snow when he heard Marc add, "We'll need a full team here, too, for processing, but the girls are now Emergency Priority."

Pierre cursed again and said a prayer that they would catch up to Marina and Clothilde before Claude did.

Chapter Thirteen

"You keep shaking and looking at that thing like it's going to spit out the meaning of life," Clothilde commented dryly to the earnest young man who was, indeed, looking at what looked like some sort of clunky cell phone as if it were the source of ultimate truth in the universe. Brian Clark, Marina thought he'd introduced himself as.

"Apologies, ma'am, but I'd be more comfortable if we waited to hear back from, uh, Mr. Constantin before we headed out — even the satellite reception seems to be going in and out."

Marina thought that he must be ex-military, with the way he spoke. His soft Southern accent reminded her of some of the Marines friends that Eduardo had introduced her to over the years.

"No apologies necessary, and I respect your opinion. It's just…I think that Marina and I would really like to put some distance between us and this place."

Clothilde was at her most charming, and even Marina was dazzled by her smile.

"We'd like to get down the mountain while the road is clear," Marina added, and the poor young man looked nearly bowled over.

"Well, I suppose that *does* make sense," he acknowledged.

"Also, didn't Marc and Pierre seem pretty eager for us to leave?" Clothilde continued, and she was only stating the facts, but the truth of her statement felt like it pierced Marina's chest. Pierre had absolutely been more than eager for them to leave, even after everything she'd told him—after what had been, for her, transcendent lovemaking.

Clark nodded haltingly. "All right, then."

Marina smiled gratefully at Clothilde, knowing that other woman had been so insistent because Marina couldn't wait to get away from the Gaspard family lodge. They had already said an affectionate good-bye to Bonnie and George, so they were able to hop into one of the large SUVs that the Gaspards kept for their use or the use of the caretakers at the lodge. Clothilde insisted on driving, which surprised Marina.

The other woman smiled and shrugged, answering the question that Marina wouldn't have been rude enough to ask out loud. "After my car accident, I was terrified to drive for a while—couldn't get into any vehicles. But Marc convinced me I wasn't helping my recovery, and that I should face my fear as often as possible until it didn't scare me anymore." Her voice went soft when she mentioned the security agent. "I hate to admit it, but he was right. Now I still drive all the time... I don't feel actively afraid anymore, although it's always there, crouched and waiting to take me over again. But I won't let it."

Marina had already liked Annelise's future sister-in-law, but her admiration swelled at the steely determination she heard in Clothilde's tone. Pierre's sister was young, beautiful and absurdly wealthy. No one would have batted an eyelash if she'd wanted to use a driver for the rest of her life or even if she wanted to stay at home and be pampered by domestic staff around the clock for a few more years. Like her brothers, though, it seemed that Clothilde had a deep pride and will.

"Be my guest," Marina offered. "Last time I drove, I ran into a huge tree trunk in a blizzard."

"I'll keep an eye on things from the back and see if we get more reception down the mountain," Clark surprised her by agreeing as well. Then again, Marina thought Clothilde was technically his boss, so maybe she kind of had to agree.

"It's no Beauxrêves, but there's a nice luxury ski lodge just before we get to the next town. They have an amazing old-fashioned cider museum nearby that sells the best maple candy. We could head there?"

Marina felt an unreasonable irritation, bordering on anxiety. She had really hoped to get far enough away from Beauxrêves Lodge and Pierre Gaspard that she could work on starting to forget everything about him and her time there — which would only take, oh, about a hundred years or so.

"Does that sound like a plan?" Clothilde asked, turning to look at her as they began their slow descent down the well-plowed road. The sky looked gray again, though, and flurries were just starting to swirl around the sturdy vehicle.

Marina sighed. "I don't suppose we can make it to Boston instead? Or even halfway?"

Clothilde looked sympathetic. "Not with another storm moving in. There's no way we should take the helicopter for a while and driving through the mountains will be too challenging." She looked thoughtful. "We do have a house in Maine. It's a converted lighthouse."

"Of course you do," Marina teased, and it felt good to joke about something.

Clothilde laughed, and the silvery sound rolled through the quiet vehicle. "I guess we are a little over-the-top, huh? If you grow up this way, it just feels...normal. I meant that we could try to head straight east instead. It would take a few hours, but it could be an easier drive. That is, if we can make it out of the mountains again before the storm gets worse."

"I mean, I had my heart set on curling up with Annelise's cat and some fancy ice cream I stashed for emergency use only, so either of your suggestions are really going to cramp my style," Marina answered dryly—and surprised a laugh out of Clark, too.

She tried to be logical, though. Her heart might be telling her that she needed to flee far away from The Asshole, as she'd mentally decided to call Pierre henceforth, but reason dictated that traveling extra distances in snowstorms was probably not the best plan.

She sighed, hating that she felt the need to be reasonable. "Much as I am dying to check out your lighthouse—"

"Oh, it's been decommissioned," Clothilde clarified. "No light anymore...just for show."

Marina laughed again. "Right, of course. I would love to see your decommissioned former lighthouse someday, but it seems crazy to drive a few unnecessary hours in an advancing snowstorm just so I can escape from your brother."

The grimace looked wrong, somehow, on Clothilde's face. "He's my brother, and I love him, but he was...harsh."

Marina cut her off before she could say anything else. "We don't have to talk about it."

Clothilde nodded. "Sure, of course...just, I would have been willing to go all *Thelma and Louise* with you."

"Um, didn't *Thelma and Louise* die at the end?" Clark's drawl from the back seemed to surprise them both, as if they'd forgotten his presence.

"Curve ball from the bleachers! I'm surprised a young man such as yourself would admit to knowing so much about a classic chick flick." Clothilde's joking words made Marina's heart feel a little bit lighter.

"I have three older sisters, ma'am," Clark replied.

"Ah," Clothilde imbued the one little sound with a wealth of comprehension, and Marina caught his eye in the rear-view mirror and smiled.

"Can we call you Brian? Would you mind? We can talk about how you ended up so far from home as we head to that luxury resort down the mountain."

"They didn't tell Bonnie and George where they were headed, and we're still not able to pull them up from GPS or on Clark's sat phone."

Marc's report wasn't unexpected, but that didn't make it any less frustrating to Pierre. In addition to his worry and exasperation, he had begun to have an uncomfortable sensation that maybe he'd miscalculated on more than just Marina and Clothilde being safer from Claude away from him. Even as they'd snowmobiled over to the main lodge and thrown a couple of bags of precautionary supplies together, he had unwillingly replayed the scenes with Marina over and over in his head.

What if she hadn't meant that she was thinking of Jaime? But then again, what the hell else could she have meant? Should he have listened to her? He knew he'd thought it was best for her to be away as soon as possible. He was the head of an enormous company, its accompanying financial empire, and also the head of the Gaspard family and staff. He wasn't used to being challenged. That was what he told himself most days, anyway. But really, what if he just didn't like it, and almost everyone else around him let him get away with it? What kind of a man did that make him? As he double-checked the contents of one of the go-bags from the lockbox in the garage, the recognition hit him that maybe he'd just acted the way he'd sworn he would try not to with Marina simply from wounded pride and bruised ego.

"*Merde, alors,*" he said out loud. Marc grunted next to him.

"If that was in reference to continued radio silence from Clark and the girls" — his acting head of security's accent was thick, and the name of the other man sounded like '*Clahk*' — "then I agree. If you were just realizing that yes, you were a total ass to Marina Lopez, then I also couldn't agree more."

Marc's irreverent comments surprised a snort of laughter from Pierre. He looked at the other man, not for the first time seeing a battle-hardened warrior —

scarred and harsh, but also fucking brilliant. "You're a terrible employee, did you know that?"

Marc grinned, unperturbed. "Good thing I don't really work for you, then, isn't it?" He heaved the last bag into the cargo area of the massive SUV, which was built like a tank, and closed the liftgate.

"Good thing," Pierre agreed, raising one eyebrow. "Now let's get the hell on the road before the snow gets any heavier again. I have a feeling about where they might have gone."

"You were right," Marina called out to Clothilde as she made her way from her bath in the massive, jetted tub upstairs. "I so needed that bath, desperately." The robe the resort had provided was thick Egyptian cotton and felt like heaven against her skin. The slippers were silky but padded, like walking on clouds. Her emotions might be bruised and battered right down to her core, but at least she felt clean and warm. Clothilde had experience with heartbreak and pain, so Marina had listened when the other woman had suggested that she needed a long bath.

"Clothilde?" Marina called out again. When she had gone to the upstairs bathroom of the good-sized cottage, Clothilde had gone to the downstairs one, while Brian had insisted on patrolling the perimeter outside. "Hey, did you fall asleep?" she added, partly to herself. She didn't want to voice the suggestion too loudly or their overeager guard might come running in to try to rescue her. Funny, but Brian and Clothilde were probably the same age. Clothilde just had a sadness about her eyes that made her seem older. No, older wasn't the right word. She seemed wise beyond her years, though.

"Clothilde?" she called again. "You'd better answer or Brian is going to come charging in any second," she joked.

"Oh, he won't be charging anywhere for a while," a strange voice whispered into her ear, making her scream, which was cut off as a hand clamped down over her mouth so hard that she tasted blood.

Chapter Fourteen

Her first thought was fear for what the intruder might have done to Clothilde, but as she struggled against the strong arm that locked around her waist, she saw the other woman tied to one of the kitchen chairs, also dressed in her bathrobe. Her second thought was for Brian. She prayed that he hadn't been hurt too badly.

"Marina Lopez," the man's creepy voice continued next to her ear, with an unmistakable French accent. "I have seen you from a distance, and in pictures, but up close, you really are quite superb. It's no wonder the great Pierre Gaspard is so taken with you." He giggled, as if in response to a joke. "Or should I say, *has* taken you?"

She tried to kick and twist, but his grip seemed freakishly strong as he dragged her toward the chair set close to Clothilde's. "You were quite loud this morning, you know? Rude. Common. Not like Clothilde here. My fiancée was always exceedingly ladylike in everything she did." He paused casually, as if he weren't holding a struggling woman in his arms. "I suppose you can't really be blamed, though, since you didn't know I was there, hiding in the closet."

Marina, already panicked by the surprise attack, was experiencing a deep feeling of revulsion mingled with flat-out horror at the idea that this man, obviously Claude de Voltin, had been hidden upstairs while she and Pierre had slept, then while they'd made love.

She bit his hand and he yelped in pain, releasing her enough that she could wiggle out of his grip. She dove for the chair where Clothilde was bound, with an idea of untying her friend, but instead she felt the weight of the man land on top of her, and she tasted more blood and saw stars flicker in her vision as her temple slammed against the tile floor.

"*Salope!*" He spat out the insult. "I was going to tie you to a chair like a civilized person — a *lady* — but now you don't deserve more than lying here on the floor," he continued, digging his knee into her back. She whimpered in spite of her best efforts to hold the sound in.

"No need to hold back… I like hearing screams of pain, and it's been too long." Claude twisted his hand into her hair, forcing her to gasp and her eyes to water. Something in his voice made her stomach turn over and heave. Through her wobbly vision, she saw Clothilde. The other woman looked furious at Claude and sympathetic toward Marina. But she also looked intent on conveying something, in spite of the gag wrapped around her mouth. Marina narrowed her eyes, ignoring the searing pain in her scalp. Yes, Clothilde was darting her eyes at the counter, where they had left three tall glasses from the ice water they'd drunk when they'd arrived.

"Have you…done this often?" she struggled to ask, not being able to draw a deep breath with Claude's weight on top of her.

"I'm sure you're just stalling, but I'll indulge you." His laugh was a creepy parody of a polite chuckle. "Especially since I think I'll have plenty of time with both of you before anyone can guess where you are." Marina felt a shiver of revulsion. He paused thoughtfully. "I've only done what I had to do, to avenge my father and my family."

She wanted to disagree emphatically and tell Claude that he was certifiably insane, but she also wanted to get a chance to grab a glass from the counter and shatter it to make a weapon.

"It makes sense. The Gaspards took your father and fortune from you, so you had to take revenge." She tried to sound as reasonable as possible while crushed to the kitchen floor underneath a homicidal maniac. She must have done a passable job, or Claude just didn't care, because he nodded.

"Not just our fortune—but our standing! Our reputation! They made my father die a fool, a laughingstock. Pierre Gaspard did that. Nothing more precious to him than his family—everyone knows that—well, apparently, his family and you." He twisted her hair again and her vision grew hazy for a second.

"It was such fun, knowing that they all loved me, that his stupid bitch of a sister even agreed to marry me—as if I would ever want her." Clothilde made a noise from across the room, but Marina couldn't tell if it were out of hurt or rage.

"All the while, M—" He caught himself. "My partner and I were building a criminal empire right under their noses. We planned to continue for a while longer, but the Ice Queen over there couldn't stand the idea of me being with another woman who wasn't a cold fish, so we had to move up phase two of our plan."

"Murdering the Gaspards?" Marina prompted, trying to keep the horror out of her voice, waiting for any slackening in his grip.

The corners of his mouth twisted down, and Marina could see that Claude must have once been considered a very handsome man.

"Murder is such an *ugly* word. Let's say 'eliminate'." He tut-tutted. "Now, we've talked long enough. Let's get you tied up nice and tight."

As he rose off her slightly to reach for the rope, she saw her chance and put every ounce of energy she had into moving out from underneath him, rolling and standing at the same time with all the strength her arms and legs could muster. She only dimly heard his roar of rage, intent on making it to the glasses on the nearby counter in spite of her wobbly balance. She reached out and nearly had one in her hand when Clothilde gave a muffled cry of alarm before Claude's entire weight slammed into her for the second time.

The glass shattered and her head thumped first against the granite countertop, then again onto the pristine tile floor. She expected to feel his weight come down onto her, but instead, in a mind that was going hazier by the second, there was what could only be described as a war cry. It was so primal that goosebumps rose all over her skin, but she couldn't seem to get her muscles to move so she could look toward where it came from. Somehow, it also sounded anguished.

A huge commotion was going on—she could tell that much—but even as she tried to stay alert, her mind drifted more and more. The pain in her head, scalp, arms, knees...all of it faded, and she saw a dazzling array of memory after memory, almost as if she'd lived them all again in the space of an instant—eating ice cream and watching movies with Annelise and laughing until their bellies hurt, learning how to make hot cocoa from her nana, adding just the right blend of spices to make it special, so real she could almost smell and taste it, running toward Eduardo when he came home from his last deployment, hugging him so tightly that she could have burst with relief and pride, dancing with Jaime near the bonfire on the beach, feeling the cool weight of his engagement ring on her finger and filled to the brim with joy.

Then her mind abruptly centered in on Pierre's harsh, handsome features, smiling at her—gruff, tender, passionate—and something snapped into place inside her. *Love.* She saw *love* on his face, as great as the love she felt for him in return. She didn't know how it had happened in such a short time, or exactly when, but she'd fallen in love with the tough, beautiful man. She should have told him, should have insisted on explaining, but she could do it now. She *had* to do it. She struggled to keep her mind together, to stay and see what was going on around her, but something bumped into her stomach with a flash of white-hot agony and everything faded to black.

Pierre thought he had known regret. Pain. Loss. But as he watched Claude slamming Marina's head into the stone countertop then onto the floor while they approached from outside, knowing he was too far away to get there in time to stop it, he felt an overwhelming torment and rage overtake him, unlike anything he'd ever known. If only they'd been quicker, driving faster, convincing the clerk at the front desk to tell them where to find the girls and Clark...but they hadn't. As he watched the ugly scene play out in front of them, it looked as if it were in slow motion. Then he realized that he was running, and Marc and Barnes were right there with him, not trying to stop him as he burst into the cabin with a guttural scream of fury that burned through his much-abused vocal cords.

Claude's look of surprise would have been comical if it hadn't been such a serious situation. The escaped criminal had clearly planned to take his time — Pierre shuddered to imagine what he would have done — and hadn't been expecting them to find him almost immediately. As he barreled into the man he'd once considered like a third brother, he felt a satisfying thud as Claude's body and head hit the ground, away from Clothilde and Marina.

Something like a red haze had fallen over Pierre's vision, making him both hyperaware of every detail around him but also unable to focus on anything but stopping Claude, on incapacitating him. How *dared* he go after Pierre's family again? And an innocent woman? Pierre realized with stark certainty, maybe too late, that his feelings for said '*innocent woman*' might go much deeper than he'd realized.

If he'd hoped that Claude would go down easily, though, he would have been disappointed. Out of the corner of his eye, Pierre saw that Marc had finished untying Clothilde with surprisingly gentle hands, but

Marina still lay motionless. He was so distracted by his concern that he almost missed Claude's jumping back to his feet like some sort of demented jackrabbit. He would have missed it, in fact, if not for Barnes yelling a warning.

As it was, Claude still caught him in the jaw with a glancing blow, but Pierre pushed aside the pain in his body and focused on his former friend. Disconcertingly, Claude was smiling, although a thin trickle of blood leaked from one corner of his mouth from his earlier fall.

"I was hoping you'd find us, although not so soon. You ruined my surprise." He had maneuvered himself into a decent defensive position, crouching in the corner with a sliding door behind him and Marina next to him. Unless Pierre wanted to risk him injuring Marina more, it would be difficult for Pierre, Marc and Barnes to take him down, in spite of the weapons they'd brought. Difficult, but not impossible, and Pierre could feel the other two men moving into position. Claude obviously saw their movements too, and his eyes flickered like steel before his grin grew wider. With the blood in his mouth, his normally white, even teeth were stained an eerie pink.

"Maybe you'll take me back to jail, maybe not. It's not like you'll keep me there." He glanced again, lightning fast, at Marc, his expression turning cunning. "I think I still accomplished most of what I wanted to, though. Almost destroying your precious little frigid bitch of a sister was good — *non*, it was *fantastique* — but murdering the woman you're too stupid to realize you're in love with before you can even tell her? That's *way* better."

Every cell in Pierre's body felt like it cried out at once as Claude's intent became clear, and Pierre saw the glint of the dim light off of a large piece of glass that Claude must have picked up from the floor and concealed in one bloody hand. Pierre lunged forward but feared he would be too late as the man's hand connected with Marina's abdomen. He hadn't counted on Marc's speed, though, or that the former war hero and Barnes would somehow have been able to coordinate with each other silently. The two other men moved with dizzying speed, Marc flying from his position to kick-tackle Claude away from Marina to where Barnes waited, a knife appearing almost out of thin air into his hand, to quickly restrain Claude.

Pierre dimly heard his sister exclaim, "Marc!" He couldn't tear his eyes away from Marina's still form, though. She had groaned when Claude had touched her, but then had gone limp again, and she looked alarmingly pale. There was a dark red stain spreading on her stomach through the thick bathrobe, and she had dark bruises already rising on her temple and her cheek that would probably be ugly—if she survived long enough to care. His heart felt like it twisted in his chest and he knelt next to her, trying to avoid the rest of the broken glass, and was about to take off his sweater and t-shirt to use them to put some sort of pressure on her wound when Clothilde appeared next to him with a first-aid kit. He raised his eyebrows in appreciation of her resourcefulness.

"Thanks, *Clochette*," he said, using the childhood nickname for his sister, but only managing a hoarse whisper through his torn and aching vocal cords. "Hope you're okay. Marina doesn't—" His voice cracked. "She doesn't look good."

Clothilde gave a short nod of understanding. "I'll do whatever I can to help you," she said simply, crouching down and gingerly exposing the bleeding slash on Marina's soft skin. She swabbed away the blood around the area with a large sterile pad of some sort. "Marc is holding on to, uh, the prisoner." Her voice held hurt when she spoke about Claude, but then she appeared to give herself a mental shake. "Barnes is calling the police on his sat phone and going to find Brian…Brian Clark." Her voice held deep worry as she handed him sanitizing wipes for his hands, then another good-sized, clean gauze pad.

"Help should be here soon, but in the meantime, we don't have to worry about being interrupted."

Pierre winced as he applied light pressure on Marina's jagged cut, and his stomach twisted into a tight knot when she didn't so much as twitch. "I'm most worried about her head. It looked like she hit it hard several times," he ground out, and his sister worked with him, deftly applying surgical tape around the gauze pad.

"She…*has* to be okay," he whispered, almost more to himself than his sister. He stroked one finger lightly down her velvety cheek. "Do you hear that, *bébé*? You stay with me now. I *command* it." He spoke low, but the words felt torn from someplace deep inside him that he hadn't wanted to bring back to life, ever—the place Marina had awoken in spite of him.

A blast of icy air and snowflakes blew in through the sliding door as Barnes, with a very weak- and injured-looking Clark leaning heavily on him, staggered into the cabin.

"The police should be here as soon as possible," Barnes announced. "I told them we could hold the package for as long as necessary. ETA on the chopper is three minutes, and they're calling the closest trauma hospital."

Pierre was stunned, but a glimmer of hope rose in his chest. He would pay or do anything—anything at all—to get Marina to a hospital. "That's amazing, but...where the hell did you find a pilot crazy enough to fly in this weather?"

Barnes looked impassive, but his eyes flashed toward Marc for just a split-second.

"An old friend of mine owed me a favor," Marc answered gruffly.

"If...no, *when* Marina is out of danger, you and your friend can name anything of mine and it will be yours," he vowed. His sister and Marc exchanged a look, the kind of intimate look reserved for close friends and lovers. Normally he would have cared, but now he just didn't give a damn about anything but Marina.

It looked like they'd stopped the bleeding of her cut, which was good, but she still hadn't stirred. He brushed the hair off her face, feeling the silky strands slide through his fingers just as they had a few hours earlier, but he'd been too much of a goddamn ass to appreciate it. To fully appreciate *her*. So what if she still loved her fiancé? Wasn't he man enough to handle that she had a past? That she'd cared deeply for someone else? Pierre vowed in that moment to make things right. She might not forgive him, might never want to be with him again, but he would make sure she was taken care of.

As he looked down at the still, pale form of his fierce little warrior, who had been so brave as to try to rescue herself and Clothilde from a madman, he recognized the softening in his chest for what it was. Maybe he'd figured it out too late, but he loved her, was deeply, madly in love with her. He only prayed he might someday have the chance to tell her—not that he deserved it.

Chapter Fifteen

Marina didn't want to get up yet. She was having the most beautiful dream, and it felt important. More than a dream, it started off as a memory, one she'd all but forgotten.

She was on the beach with Jaime, on an old plaid blanket. He was sitting with his back against a large, round boulder, weathered by time and waves, and he cradled her head in his lap. He stroked her hair with gentle fingers.

"Mi corazón, if I don't come back —"

Marina interrupted him. "You're coming back!" she ordered fiercely.

Jaime's smile was tender. "Always, Marinita. Always, in spirit if in no other way." He paused. "But if something does happen, I want you to promise me something."

"I don't want to promise to go on without you or anything ridiculous like that. I don't think I could be happy without you, missing a piece of my heart, a piece of my soul." She sat up, and a tear rolled down her cheek. "Do you have to go back? I have a bad feeling."

Jaime held her hand tightly. "I believe what we're doing is right, making the world a better place and a safer place for you and your grandmother, my parents and my brothers and sisters. Don't ask me to give that up, honey."

She swiped at her tears with the back of her hand and forced a smile. It was true. She loved Jaime and this was part of what made him the wonderful man he was. "No...no, I would never do that. And I'm proud of you. So very proud."

His smile warmed her all the way to her bones. "Thank you. Truly. Now give me a different promise, then."

"Anything," she answered promptly, and he chuckled.

"You don't even know what I'm going to ask, you goose!"

She shrugged. "It doesn't matter. I'll agree. I trust you completely."

"If there ever comes a time when I'm not around anymore, I want you to stay joyful, hopeful and open. Just...stay yourself. Can you promise me that, at least?"

Marina hesitated, not really wanting to imagine a world that could ever not hold Jaime, but she nodded reluctantly. "Yes, for you, yes. I promise."

The memory, which should have continued to them kissing and talking then wading into the cold water together seemed to end – but the dream continued.

"You didn't always keep your promise," dream-Jaime chided gently. "But I forgive you, mi corazón."

Tears stung her eyes. He felt so real, like she could reach out and touch him.

"You can't, honey. I'm not really here. But I just wanted to tell you that it's okay."

She swallowed. "What's okay?"

His face looked so young, but his expression was patient. "You know what. Giving him things you never gave me, feeling differently. Caring for him. You don't need my permission, but you have it. Always. I love you too much to want anything other than your happiness."

Marina didn't know what woke her, but Jaime's image slowly faded away, and she became aware first of a strong antiseptic smell that burned her nostrils. There were periodic beeps and whirrs, and she blinked against a harsh, over-bright light that seared her eyes and made her squeeze them shut more tightly.

"I think she's in pain. She's crying," someone was rumbling in a worried, gravelly voice. A voice she...loved? She was confused, but the sound of that man comforted her.

"...on that strong a painkiller, as you insisted, she is truly feeling a minimum of pain, but I can give her a little bit more."

Something warm closed around her hand... *His hand*, she realized, and his voice got closer.

"I don't know if you can hear me, but I'm sorry, *bébé*. So sorry. For the way I treated you, for putting you in danger, but most of all for not being there in time to protect you. Maybe you can't forgive me, but I'm too much of an arrogant asshole not to fight for you."

She wanted to laugh and to cheer. Pierre Gaspard was whispering his version of sweet nothings into her ear, and he was absolutely terrible at it, but everything he said made her heart warm in her chest. Unfortunately, she couldn't seem to pry her eyes open again, though, and the real world faded back into the background one more time.

Still, she managed to whisper his name.

Pierre wasn't certain he'd ever felt such a mixture of elation and concern. She'd said his name! They'd told him days ago that she had come out of the medically-induced coma that the experts had advised as they relieved the swelling in her brain, but she'd still been resting continuously, so he hadn't truly believed them. He had barely slept in the days since the attack at the cabin, and he hadn't left her bedside. He'd had an irrational fear that if he left, she might slip away, so he'd stayed, talking to her constantly. Reassuring her. Apologizing. He barely knew what he was saying anymore. So...now that she might have actually heard him, he was a little abashed. The great Pierre Gaspard, renowned for being a charming playboy, and the best he could come up with was, *'I'm an arrogant asshole?'* She knew that already. He should have been telling her he loved her, needed her, missed her every second of every day.

When his brother Rémy put his hand on Pierre's shoulder, he nearly levitated out of his chair with shock.

"You need to get some rest, *Pierrot*. You look like shit."

Luc, his youngest brother, sidled up next to Rémy and looked pained. "Hate to agree with this smug SOB, but you smell like shit, too." Luc, who was the head of the European branch of Gaspard Industries, had already been back in North America from his usual residence in Paris for the engagement party and had extended his stay.

"What is this, an intervention?" Pierre asked, half-jokingly. His brothers' faces were serious.

"Yes," Rémy agreed. "That's exactly what this is."

"We know you want to impress Marina and get her to forgive whatever stupid thing you did which, from how *Clochette* tells it, was pretty damn bad." His youngest brother smiled with evil glee. "But sitting here nearly unconscious with over a week's worth of beard and clothes that you've only changed once isn't going to help. If we hadn't donated an obscene amount of money to this hospital, they would have kicked you out themselves long ago."

"I'm not leaving," he answered. He knew he sounded childishly stubborn, but he didn't care. He was the head of the goddamned family and he didn't need advice from his younger brothers.

Rémy sighed. "I told you we'd have to bring in the big guns."

Luc made a face. "You were right... I should have listened to you. He's even further gone than I realized."

Pierre tried to tune out his brothers' banter — and he was sure that Clothilde would have been there, too, if she hadn't gone to Boston with Marc to take care of things with Claude — but something caught his attention. "The big guns?"

With a warm vanilla smell and a smile that always seemed to reach out and hug everyone around her, Annelise, his soon-to-be sister-in-law, stepped into the room. "I think he means me," she answered apologetically.

"*You're* the big guns?" he scoffed, then, to his surprise, his brother's normally easy-going fiancée transformed into a fire-breathing she-dragon who could probably eat lesser men for breakfast. Or at least, a very persuasive friend who made him feel terrible. He *was* extremely tired, after all.

"Yes, I am...and I'll tell you why. That's my best friend you're sitting next to. The woman I have known since we were little kids, playing dress-up and make-believe with dolls. Ever since she was six years old, Marina has been smart, funny, kind and deeply giving to all those around her. She lost her mom, her dad and the love of her young life, but she kept going, still spreading her own special brand of love and happiness to the world. To *me*." She paused, but he thought it was only to take a breath. "I heard that you said some terrible things to her, and honestly, I don't really care if you want to sit here and marinate in a miasma of stinky clothes and regret, but Marina deserves better."

She poked him in the chest and he looked down at her finger wonderingly, seeing for the first time that the kitten had claws. "I love your brother," she said forcefully.

"Thanks, *chérie*. Love you, too," Rémy interjected, having the nerve to sound amused.

"Don't interrupt a good tirade!" she complained, and Rémy raised his hands placatingly.

"So sorry, my Annelise. You're doing so beautifully," Rémy encouraged.

Annelise glared at her fiancé, but her expression held tenderness.

"As I was saying, I love your brother, and he seems to think that you're a great guy. I have my reservations, but I'm willing to trust him. So I'm going to be completely honest. You need to take a shower and a nap, in that order, before you even attempt to apologize to Marina, or grovel, prostrate yourself, whatever. I recommend all three." She waved her hand in the air, nearly hitting him in the face, and he hid a surprised smile.

Still, he wasn't going anywhere. "I appreciate your honesty," he started. "But I don't want to leave this hospital."

"That's why we came prepared," Luc answered, a set of clothes seeming to materialize in his hand. Obviously, he'd been holding them behind his back, and Pierre was just too bleary-eyed and fuzzy to notice.

"You can shower here and they are going to bring in a cot from the maternity ward for you to sleep on." Rémy continued.

"I, uh, that's…" Pierre was speechless at his family's kindness. "I don't know where to begin," he said.

Luc and Rémy exchanged a look.

"You could start by trusting us a little bit more. You may have had to do everything for us when we were younger and take on the burdens for our whole family, but we're grown-ups now. Real adults. Let *us* help *you* sometimes, too." Luc spoke gently, lightly, but Pierre could tell he meant the words — that it really mattered to him.

Pierre wanted to blame being overtired, which he certainly was, but he felt a tightness in his throat at Luc's words that had nothing to do with exhaustion and everything to do with the swell of love and pride he felt in his brothers.

"Thank you," he answered simply. "We can talk about this more later, but for now, I believe someone suggested I should take a shower and a nap…in that order."

Chapter Sixteen

The unmistakable scent of her best friend's favorite perfume teased her nose and a grin spread across her face before she even opened her eyes. As she dragged them open to slits, the light was dimmer, more comfortable than before.

"Anna," she croaked, and her closest friend's face materialized into her line of vision as her eyes adjusted.

"Rina!" Annelise exclaimed in a hushed tone, but joyfully in spite of that. "You've been stirring, even enough that we could get you to drink a little bit of water, which the doctors were happy with, but not really waking up. Pierre has an army of them taking care of you. How are you feeling?"

It was so wonderful to see and hear her best friend that tears welled up.

"Oh no! Is it really painful?" Annelise looked deeply worried, a little wrinkle appearing between her eyebrows.

Marina shook her head, regretting the motion as soon as she did. "No… I mean, yes, it's painful, but only a little. That's not why I'm crying. It's so good to see you. I missed you, lots."

Annelise hugged her gently. "Me too! So much! Gosh, we were so worried about you." She released her with a little squeeze.

"What happened with Claude? Is Clothilde okay?"

Annelise nodded reassuringly. "Clothilde is fine. Just a little banged up, but nothing serious at all. As I understand it, Marc, Pierre and Tim Barnes all worked together to take Claude down in the cabin and he's fully recaptured. According to Marc, he's now under 'extreme security measures', whatever that means." She paused and looked fierce. "What I hope it means is that the bastard never gets out again to try to hurt someone else."

Something loosened in Marina's chest and she felt easier, knowing that Claude was locked up again and everyone was generally okay. Well, except her.

Annelise continued. "Before I forget, your brother and your nana wanted to come, but her doctors were still firm that she can't really travel right now. Pierre set it up so they have regular video calls with your medical team, and now that you're awake, I'm sure they'll want to see you too."

It was incredibly thoughtful, and Marina felt her eyes sting again.

"Is Pierre…around? I thought I heard him earlier but…I was probably dreaming. And where is 'here' anyway?" Marina asked carefully.

Annelise obviously wasn't fooled by her casual tone, but she played along.

"We're in Burlington, which was the biggest trauma hospital nearby. Some mysterious pilot friend of Marc's flew you and Brian Clark here through the tail-end of that snowstorm, and rumor has it — well, Clothilde, really — that Pierre offered them anything at all in gratitude." Annelise looked conspiratorial.

"Oh my God, is Brian okay?" Marina asked, feeling terrible that she'd temporarily forgotten about the young man.

Her friend nodded. "Yeah, apparently just some shallow wounds and one big knock on his head, but they released him pretty quickly." She paused thoughtfully. "It all had a really hush-hush, cloak-and-dagger feeling. Almost like…I mean, it would be crazy, but…" She trailed off and refocused on Marina. "Never mind that. But Brian is totally fine. Clothilde really wanted to be here, too, but she's dealing with the Claude situation in Boston with Marc. I'm so glad you're both safe! And everyone else, too! When we heard Claude had taken you and Clothilde, I was freaking out, and I thought Rémy and Luc were going to lose their minds."

After many years of listening to Annelise's rapid-fire words, she was used to her friend's exuberant, sometimes train-of-thought style of talking, but it never ceased to amaze her. "Thanks, Anna. I'm really glad, too. It was, um, pretty awful, I'm not gonna lie. And I don't even know what happened after I got knocked out, which kind of makes it feel more sinister."

Annelise moved in closer and squeezed her shoulder very gently, reassuringly, before taking her hand. "What's the last thing you remember? *If* you want to talk about, which you totally don't have to."

Searching her memory, Marina tried to answer as completely as possible. "I had managed to wiggle out of Claude's grip and was going to get a glass as a weapon, but he..." Her voice broke. "Um, I guess knocked me down is the nice term." She touched the bandage at her temple, and winced at how tender it still felt. "I hit my head a couple times, really hard, then I was lying there on the floor and I couldn't move. I heard a lot of noise, but I just kind of floated away, especially when I felt something else..." She struggled to remember. "My stomach? I don't really know what happened much after I fell, I guess."

The death-grip that her friend had on her hand tightened even further. "It's probably not a bad thing that you don't remember clearly. Claude cut you with a shard of broken glass, so you had to get twenty-two stitches on your abdomen, but it could have been much worse. Clothilde said that Pierre stormed in like some sort of avenging angel initially to throw Claude off you, then—her description—Marc flew through the air like he belonged in a kung fu movie to kick Claude away from you when he was cutting you. Still, if you hadn't been airlifted straight to the hospital, there's a good chance you wouldn't have made it." Her voice wobbled.

Marina drew in a shaky breath, which sounded loud amid all the quiet beeps and swishes of the hospital room. "That makes sense, because...I think I saw Jaime."

Her friend gasped. "You did? Oh my gosh, with a bright light? Then he was waiting with open arms but he told you to go back, that it wasn't your time? Were your parents there?"

Marina laughed out loud, grimacing at how much such a simple act could hurt her entire body. "No! You are watching too many chick flicks, *chica*! It wasn't like that. It was more like a memory, but then we spoke. It was…so real. And he told me everything with Pierre was okay."

Her best friend's expression filled with interest. "And what *is* everything with Pierre? He's been… I don't think 'frantic' begins to describe how worried he's been about you. He obviously cares about you, but there's something else, too."

Marina groaned and closed her eyes. "Oh, Anna, I couldn't stand him, but I still liked him. Then when we were trapped together, everything was pretty much amazing. But after we, uh, you know, made love, I was crying—"

"Um, *what*?" Annelise interjected. "*Crying* doesn't sound amazing."

Marina tried to explain. "I know… I was just overwhelmed by the experience, and I felt bad for being so happy. No, more like *blown away* with satisfaction. Then I said Jaime's name and Marc burst in before I had a chance to explain."

Annelise clucked sympathetically, somehow making the sound, usually the exclusive purview of older ladies, sound completely natural coming from her.

"Then Pierre said the ugliest things to me, to get me to leave, but I thought he was probably lashing out…then, well, you kinda know the rest," she finished lamely.

"Okay, I have been waiting *so long* to give you advice about someone who might actually be worthy of you, not just one of the jerks you were going out with because you knew they'd be safe since they'd never touch your heart."

"Fair point...you always said that, and I never listened, but I think you were right," Marina agreed.

"I don't know how things will turn out, but I can only tell you that I took a risk with Rémy — a lot of risks, actually — and it was totally worth it. I threw aside my pride and so did he, and I have never, ever been happier." Anna's voice dropped. "More important, though, even if it hadn't worked out, when it looked like it might not go anywhere at all and he hurt me, deeply, I was so grateful that I had tried. That I had taken the chance. I would have regretted it for the rest of my life, just like you told me, if I hadn't."

Marina could see how happy her closest friend was, how deeply in love, and anyone who looked at Rémy could tell he felt the same way.

"I'm willing to risk it, Anna, but I don't know if he is," she whispered.

Her friend raised one eyebrow. "That man hasn't left your side since you came here. He fought a dangerous criminal for you, then has been using the entirety of influence his station can buy to get you the best care, the best everything. Heck, we practically had to knock him out to get him to take a shower and a nap. I think Luc might have been holding a syringe of sedative behind his back. He's a wily one. Even so, Pierre is in the adjoining room, sleeping like the dead on a cot because he refused to go any farther away from you, and he's going to be royally pissed that he missed your waking up." Again, she paused for what Marina suspected was only to breathe. "If actions speak louder than words, Rina, *he's* willing to try."

Whatever else Annelise might have said was interrupted by the arrival of a nurse, who called in a doctor as well, and they seemed incredibly pleased with her progress.

An hour later, having been thoroughly examined, poked and prodded, she was shocked by how exhausted she was just from doing practically nothing. Still, the little bit of extra effort to have Annelise help her brush her teeth and dry-shampoo and brush her long hair had made her feel more human again.

She felt more than heard Pierre in the doorway of the room. His tall silhouette, so elegant but also strong, leaning against the utilitarian white hospital doorframe, nearly took her breath away.

"It's not like Pierre Gaspard to hesitate in doorways," she said, trying for a light tone but only managing to sound hoarse.

"True...but that's only who I play on TV. This guy"—he motioned with one thumb at himself—"is just appreciating that you look so much better."

She gave a tremulous smile. "Annelise helped, but it is nice not to feel like the Bride of Frankenstein who had a mouse crawl into her mouth and die."

His bark of laughter was surprised and echoed in the now-quiet room, since they'd been able to turn off a lot of the noisier machines. When he stepped into the room, the harsh light hit the planes of his face. He was still handsome—Lord knew, there would never come a time when he wasn't handsome—but he looked tired, craggy and maybe a little older.

"You have such a way with words, *Marinette*," he answered, his voice rich and low—but scratchier than she remembered.

"Did you damage your vocal cords again?" she asked.

He nodded reluctantly, and his eyes were intense. "It doesn't matter, though. It was worth it."

"Annelise told me that you knocked Claude off me. I don't even know how to begin to thank you," she said, and there was a flicker of pain in his eyes, quickly gone. "I thought I might have heard you in here earlier?" She made the statement a question.

His shoulders heaved as he took a deep breath and sat down on the chair next to her. She'd thought perhaps Annelise had pulled it up, but something about the easy way that Pierre maneuvered into the spot told her that maybe he'd moved it there, had been spending a lot of time sitting in it.

"I was here," he confirmed. "You shouldn't thank me, *bébé*." His voice was harsh, but she knew the anger wasn't directed at her. "It was my fault you were in danger, my fault you were nearly..." His voice cracked and splintered, and when he looked at her, his eyes were shining with tears. She wouldn't have expected to see Pierre cry about much of anything. He just wasn't someone who showed emotion.

" —nearly killed," he finished hoarsely.

She tried to shake her head, but it was too painful. "No, it wasn't your fault. It was Claude's fault. He chose to follow us, knock poor Brian out and break into our cabin. *He* did that, not you."

"He honed in on you because of me, to hurt me. I should never have sent you away, right into danger." His voice sounded anguished.

"You can regret some of the things you said, if you want to, but I don't blame you for Claude's attack, and I never will. You couldn't have known." She paused and waited for him to look at her face again. "In fact, it occurs to me that with some of what you said that you might have been trying to force me to leave."

He didn't deny it. Instead, he held her gaze, and she saw deep regret, but also something warmer, much more tender. Something that gave her hope.

"Are you here just because you feel guilty?" she asked.

He brushed one strand of hair away from the bandage on her forehead with exquisite gentleness, and she nearly shivered at the contact. "*Non*," he breathed. "God forgive me, but *non, chérie*. I'm here because there isn't anywhere else that I want to be, *ever*." He searched her eyes and must have found what he was looking for, because he continued. "A better man would wait until you're recovered and take his time, be gentle and sweet, but I'm not that man, *Marinette*. I am *your* man, though. I'm so sorry for what I said, for how I acted, and I pray that you can forgive me. When I saw you, lying there so still and pale on the floor, fighting for your life, apart from terror for you, the only other thought in my mind was that I might never get the opportunity to tell you how I felt about you. I swore that if I got the chance, I would say the words, no more hesitation, because life is too precious and sometimes too damned short."

"How do you feel?" she whispered, mesmerized by the intensity of his gaze.

He gave a harsh laugh. "I feel confused, uncomfortable, oddly enchanted and wildly turned-on by almost everything you do. I love you so much, Ms. Lopez, that I can barely see straight."

As romantic declarations went, it was abysmal. Marina loved it. Once again, her eyes stung with tears, and he looked alarmed.

"You weren't supposed to cry," he said, sounding accusing. "I was prepared to have you throw me out, but...*bébé*, I never wanted to hurt you, never want to hurt you again."

"I'm not going to throw you out," she answered, and a couple of tears spilled over and rolled down her cheeks.

He looked skeptical.

"No, really. It's just that I wanted to tell you the same thing. I promised myself, when Claude was holding us captive, that if I ever had the chance, I would make you let me explain why I was crying after we, um, made love—would tell you how I felt about you."

The naked hope on his face made her heart beat faster in her chest.

"You did?" he asked.

She reached out her hand and he cradled it immediately with his, warm and strong, hard with calluses, but so caring, just like the man himself.

"I love you, too," she said, and the grin that flashed across his face felt like it spread a warm glow throughout the entire room—or maybe just throughout all of her, even into her deepest, darkest places, filling them with joy and hope instead. "I'm sorry I was crying, Pierre. I was just overcome, I think, and—"

He cut her off with a gentle finger to her lips. "You don't have to explain. I should have listened instead of assuming and getting jealous. You can tell me if you still want to—I told you before I want to hear whatever you have to say—but I want you to know you don't have to." He squeezed her hand. "I thought about it a lot, while I was sitting here, incredibly grateful your chest was rising and falling and your heart was beating." She made a sound, and he slid his hand down her cheek, but he shook his head, silently asking her to remain quiet as he continued.

"I know you didn't want to talk about it before, but I wanted to tell you that I'm sure — absolutely *certain* — that Jaime wasn't mad that you tried to make love to him then sent him away. I'm positive that his last thought, wherever he was, was gratitude that you loved him so much. You're a gorgeous, sensuous woman, and any man you love would know that he was the luckiest man alive to have you, no matter what else he believed." He lifted her hand and kissed her palm, a long, lingering kiss that made goosebumps rise on her skin. "I should have known that expressing your sensuality might have hidden pitfalls for you, *bébé*, since you confessed that you'd felt so guilty for so long. But, *chérie*, you didn't need to, and you don't need to feel ashamed now."

He understood. He *truly* understood, and she was grateful beyond words. Coupled with her long-standing guilt about how she'd parted from Jaime and her fears that she was some sort of wanton sex maniac, even though she knew that wasn't reasonable, it had been an agonizing internal contradiction to feel so much happiness and satisfaction with Pierre, but to know that she'd never felt that, and would never give or feel that, with Jaime.

"Yes," she agreed. "I know that now, but...it might come back and surprise me again sometime."

His dark eyes seemed fathomless but filled with pure love. "I can wait, *ma Marinette*. Forever, anywhere and always, I'm yours."

Love for this man — *her* man — surged inside her and she laughed with pure happiness. His expression was indulgent, bemused.

"Usually, a man expects a different, er, reception to his romantic declaration," he said dryly, but the corners of his mouth twitched in amusement.

"I'm so happy, Pierre. You have made me so happy," she assured him fervently, and pointed at her lips expectantly.

He looked confused. "Is this an American gesture?" he asked.

She laughed again. "No, you goof. I'm not really sure how to raise my head and torso again without pain so I'm wordlessly — *alluringly*, I believe — asking you to kiss me."

His chuckle was deeply amused. "You are uniquely wonderful, *chérie*. I'll kiss you anywhere you want, whenever you want me to." He waggled his eyebrows suggestively and she thought her cheeks might crack from the force of her smile. Then he covered her mouth with his and she lost all thought of anything else.

When he sat back again, she was nearly panting, and her nipples were so hard the thin fabric of the gown she wore was nearly painful on them. She sucked in a worried breath on her next thought.

"Wait, where are we going to live? How is this going to work?"

"Ah, well, as to that… I was hopeful that you might not throw me out, so just in case, I made some arrangements. Your work is already aware that you are in the hospital, so you're on medical leave for however long you need. You're free to go anywhere, but I'm hoping you'll come to Montreal to stay with private medical staff in the room we had originally had set up for Clothilde. Um, stay with *me*, that is."

He looked so uncomfortable that she took pity on him. "I just told you that I loved you. *Yes*, I'll come stay with you while I recover," she said, and she was gratified to see the great Pierre Gaspard look sheepish. Sheepish for *her*.

"What about after that, though?" she asked.

"The other reason I want to go to Montreal is that I had a discussion with Luc just before I went to sleep. Something he said earlier made me realize that I've been, well, living in the past—the past where my siblings were kids and they needed me, and the company needed me, so I did what had to be done."

She kept quiet, waiting for whatever else he would say, which she could tell wasn't easy.

"I know they're not children—I mean, *obviously*—but Luc pointed out to me that he loved business school and loves being the head of our European operations. I've never really liked any of it. I mean, I did what was necessary, but I didn't choose it. He would be happy to transition into more responsibility, to free me up to spend time doing whatever I want. Which, as you know, is...*you, bébé*." The heat in his gaze lit a fire in her that made her squirm and catch her breath. "We can choose wherever we want to be based. Maybe Boston, to be close to Annelise and Rémy, or we could go back and forth between Boston and Montreal."

Tears rose once more at his thoughtfulness—*damn weepiness from medication and injury!*—but she pushed them down, not wanting him to misinterpret them again. "That sounds...*perfect*, Pierre." She ruined the effect a little bit by giving a huge yawn that made her jaw crack audibly, and his low laughter filled the room.

"Now sleep, I think, so you can get better," he ordered, and the firm command in his voice woke up all of her nerve endings.

"Come up here with me?" she asked.

His expression was warm and tender, but he hesitated.

"You can be really careful," she urged, and he cracked.

"Just for a minute, *chérie*," he agreed, his voice raspy, and he gingerly wedged his large frame into the uncomfortably small bed with her, assiduously avoiding all her injuries and wrapping himself around her. With a sigh of pure contentment—which might have been bliss if she hadn't still been so banged up— she fell into a deep, dreamless sleep.

Epilogue

Twelve weeks later

Pierre steeled himself to be strong, again, reminding himself that Marina's health was more important than anything else. When his resolve wavered, he just pictured her, unconscious on the kitchen floor of that rented cabin, blood seeping up through her robe. If that didn't work, he forced himself to remember the harrowing helicopter ride to the hospital through swirling snow squalls, both he and Clark holding on to Marina as he'd prayed they'd get there in time. He recalled the first days of her recovery, small and pale, nearly the same color as the hospital sheets, as they'd worried she might never wake up. Even twelve weeks later, that memory still always sobered him. He'd come damned close to losing her forever. He could manage not to make love to her for a while longer.

Every day with Marina since they'd released her from the hospital in Vermont to come stay with him in

Quebec had been a fucking gift. She was warm, funny, smart and deeply caring — everything he'd seen in her and more. They spent every evening and most days together at first, walking the grounds, watching movies, swimming — as much as she was allowed — and just generally enjoying each other's company. She'd introduced him to the joy of the classic *Scooby-Doo* cartoons, and he'd taught her about the distinctly *Montrealais* sense of humor, and more generally about the deep pride he felt in being French-Canadian.

His family, particularly Rémy and Annelise, had stopped by almost daily. Marina's grandmother had even felt strong enough to come see her granddaughter, and Eduardo had been able to take another short leave. That had been a wonderful visit, although it had also led to their first argument, because Marina had flatly refused to let Pierre help with the expensive payments for her nana's nursing facility. Their passionate make-up make-out session had almost been worth it, though, and he still felt confident that he could get her to agree to a compromise at some point.

As he stood on the main front steps of his family's sprawling estate in Montreal, he took a deep breath and braced himself to push open the massive oak double-doors, behind which he knew Marina would be waiting. Since he'd gone back to work part-time a few weeks earlier, mostly to begin the transition of power to Luc, she'd gotten into the habit of flying into his arms as soon as he got home, peppering his face with kisses and nearly driving him right up to and sometimes well beyond the brink of insanity with lust.

Today, though, the entryway was open, and his heart clenched in his chest. Claude was well and truly locked up, now — Marc had seen to that with a dedication that had sometimes bordered on obsession—but they all still had the feeling that there was some unknown accomplice who remained free, someone close to his family, with surprising, powerful connections. Had someone gotten through his family's incredibly tight security, which had been beefed up considerably since the attacks in Vermont, to get to Marina? The possibility seemed remote, but *any* possibility was too much.

He rushed around the first floor, looking for her or signs of struggle, then took the stairs by twos and threes up to the second floor, nearly sprinting by the time he got to the space where Marina was staying. She wanted them to officially share a bedroom—he slept there most nights, the sweet torture of holding her without touching her excruciating—but he had refused until she was fully recovered.

Her room was dim when he got there, but he could make out the distinct, curvy lines of her shape on the bed. The relief that flooded him made his muscles almost go weak, so that he sank down onto the overstuffed chair near the window. Actually, being a little out of breath from his mad sprint probably contributed to his decision to sit down so promptly, too.

"You're here. *Dieu merci*! I was so worried, *bébé*," he panted between breaths. *Merde*, he needed to add a half hour to his daily time at their home gym. "What's wrong? Did you push yourself too hard? You need to take things easy, *chérie*."

Marina groaned. This was not going at all the way she had expected, nor the way she had planned after she'd gotten a pep talk from Annelise.

'Just get naked,' her friend had advised. *'Men lose their minds when we get naked. Just wait there with your clothes off and he's bound to forget about being careful and just jump you.'* It had sounded like great advice earlier in the afternoon, but now, it had backfired spectacularly. She'd meant to meet him at the door naked, but then she'd worried that one of the staff could walk in, even though she'd asked them all to stay out of the family rooms that afternoon, so she'd opted instead to set some mood lighting in her bedroom and wait there...and apparently nearly given the man she loved a heart attack.

"Are you in pain, *bébé*?" Pierre's voice practically vibrated with concern, and she realized that her groan of mortification had obviously given him even more of the wrong impression. "I can call the doctor," he offered.

She sat up and shook her head, holding the blanket up under her armpits so it wouldn't slip down. "No need. She came by earlier and it was all good news. She cleared me entirely. I'm now officially one hundred percent healed, except for my scar, which I'm supposed to just rub that cream on every day to help it fade faster."

Pierre looked stunned, then ecstatic, then puzzled. She'd grown very good at reading every nuance of his expressions over the past weeks, and she couldn't believe she'd thought him so stoic before. Oh, he was still gruff, and he had lost none of his intimidation factor to other people, but she'd seen behind the curtain and she knew how deeply he cared. He would never fool her again. She could probably even beat him at poker. She rather liked the idea of strip poker with Pierre.

"If you're feeling better, why are you lying in bed?" His confusion turned to interest. "*Marinette*, are your shoulders bare?"

She stifled a laugh at the abrupt about-face. "Could we play a game where you pretend that you just walked into the room and nothing else has happened since you walked through the front door?"

His chuckle was low and sexy. Well, everything about him was sexy.

"Absolutely, *bébé*. I'll play any game you want," he answered, the rasp in his voice driving her libido into overdrive, only now she could do something about it.

"That's good," she answered. "Because it's more than just my shoulders that are bare." She let the words hang in the air and was gratified to see the bulge at the juncture of his legs grow larger, so that he shifted his legs wider in the chair. His eyes went half-lidded.

"Oh yeah?" he prompted, reaching down to adjust himself, and making her tingle with anticipation of what she was about to do.

"Mm-hm," she confirmed, her voice sounding low and throaty to her own ears. "And it's hot under the covers, so I think I'm going to take them off."

He raised his eyebrows. "You should do that, *bébé*. Can't have you getting too warm. Take those blankets off now and let me see that gorgeous body again," he growled, and it felt like he was already stroking her skin with his voice.

She knelt on the bed and let the soft covers pool around her, baring her body to the cool air of the room. He stared so intently that it felt like he was drinking her in with his eyes, lingering on every part of her, making her nipples bead into hard little points, desperate for his attention. It had been so *long*.

"Fucking beautiful, *chérie*. Like a goddamn dream," he breathed reverently, palming the bulge of his cock through his pants. "I think you need to come a little closer though." His tone was a low command, one her body went crazy for. "Those pretty little nipples look like they're begging for me to suck them, hm?"

She nodded and crawled to the bottom of the bed, letting her full breasts sway under his avid attention. When she got to the foot of the bed, she slid down and kept crawling.

The sound that Pierre made in response was definite a snarl, filled with desire. "Are you sure you can crawl, *chérie*? I love it, but…"

She smiled, feeling warmed that both her gruff asshole and her sweet, tender lover were worried about her. She nodded. "I asked the doctor specifically, and she confirmed."

"You asked her if you could *crawl* on the *floor*?" His voice sounded strangled.

"Yes, and a few other things I knew you would want to be sure about," she confirmed, her tone teasing.

His chest rose and fell rapidly with his increased breathing. "I didn't imagine I could fall in love with you any more deeply, but I think I just did, *Marinette*. You look so fucking sexy." Her heart squeezed in her chest at the same time that her pussy quivered. "Wait! What other things did you ask?" he asked, the second part of her statement obviously just registering.

She smiled up at him enigmatically from where she knelt on the floor. "You'll find out," she answered, and finished crawling to him, making herself gasp as she ran her sensitive nipples along the fabric of his pants and crawled up into his lap, facing him.

He ran his fingers through her hair before guiding her head to his and slanting his mouth over hers in a kiss that made her toes curl, stroking his tongue into her mouth, then nibbling at her lips and over to her ear, then down her neck. She straightened up a little as he went until she was all the way up onto her knees, bringing her nipples right on the level with his mouth and also putting her clitoris against the hard bulge of his arousal, with only the smooth pinstripe fabric of his suit pants separating them.

"You wanted me to bring these closer, did you?" she asked, and Pierre's gaze darkened with wild desire.

"Oh yes," he confirmed almost reverently.

With a single-minded intensity, he sucked one eager nipple into his mouth and palmed her other breast, massaging and teasing it while his mouth tugged on the first, until she writhed against him. At her motion, he sucked harder and faster, and pinched the nipple he held, making her cry out again and again. The breathy mewls of her pleasure were loud in the silent room, punctuated by the rhythmic swish of the textured fabric of his trousers against the surface of the chair. She threw her head back, thrusting her breasts even closer to him. With a deep chuckle, he released her right nipple from the cavern of his mouth and turned his attention to the left one, bucking his hips up in time to the suction of his lips, driving her wild. It felt amazing, but she had other plans in mind. She paused and, with obvious reluctance, he let her pull back, releasing her breasts but tweaking them with his fingers one final time as he did, making her moan and grind her hips against him helplessly.

"You look a little warm, too," she commented, her voice breathy with arousal. "Maybe we should take some of these clothes off."

Pierre's eyes gleamed, liquid sin, in the low light of the lamp and he inclined his head. "Whatever you wish, *chérie*."

She rubbed herself against Pierre sinuously as she slid back down against him to kneel nearly at his feet and reached up to untuck his shirt and unbutton his pants, and he rushed to take off his suit jacket and tie just above her head, nearly ripping the designer clothes in his obvious haste and throwing them haphazardly onto the floor. One of the buttons of his shirt actually popped off, hitting a metallic lamp with a loud ping, as he tore that off too. She thrilled at his eagerness, but she took her time unzipping his pants, reveling in the power she held over this sexy man.

"In a hurry?" she teased.

He made an inarticulate sound of pure lust that sent an electric shock through her. "Fucking starving for you, *bébé*."

"Me too," she answered, and slid his pants and underwear down together in one smooth motion, only appreciating the massive erection that sprang free, straining toward her, for a split second before she bent her head to his lap and took as much of his length as she could into her mouth.

"*Aaaannhhghgh*," he grunted, or that was what it sounded like to her, as he flexed his hips and butt and practically shot up out of the chair, nearly bucking her off him. She thought that was a good sign, so she sucked harder, relishing the salty taste, but when she circled the base of his wide girth with both hands, the scream he gave sounded almost like it might be pain.

"Is that a good sound or a bad sound?" she asked tentatively. "I tried to learn what I could, but I've never done this before, so —"

Pierre cut her off. "*So* good, *bébé*," he groaned. "Your mouth is fucking paradise. Any better and I'd be shooting off down your throat right now. *Putain de merde*, it's even more sexy that I'm your first." He thrust his hips up again, moving his cock in her hands, the gesture seeming almost unconscious. "In fact, I don't think I can last long at all if you keep doing that, and when I come, I want it to be inside that sweet pussy. Get up and kneel on this chair, *Marinette*."

Little quakes of pleasure vibrated deep inside her channel at his words and hurried to obey. He offset the harshness of the order by helping her stand, with exquisite gentleness. He rubbed his hands up and down her legs in long, smooth strokes as she climbed and knelt in the spot he'd just left. With his hands moving over her, and feeling so aroused from their earlier kisses and his attention to her breasts that she thought that her sex was probably glistening with juices, more than ready for his entry, she was surprised when he dropped to his knees behind her.

"Been dreaming about drinking all your cream, *bébé*, until you come screaming on my face," he growled. It was all the warning she had before he licked her in one long stroke from bottom to top, making her scream with pleasure. He kneaded and lightly smacked the globes of her ass, making her yelp with shocked pleasure as he lapped at her, then thrust his tongue inside her until she was gasping and chanting his name.

"So *good*, Pierre. Oh my God, so, so good. Pierre, ah, *Pierre!*"

At her words, he went faster, humming against her clit so that she felt the vibrations as if they spread everywhere in her body. When he thrust two fingers inside her as well, she careened up and over into the shimmering expanse of pure pleasure, her cry of ecstasy muffled as she bit down on the thick fabric of the chair. He continued gentle strokes of his tongue as she rode out several aftershocks, stroking her legs as she came back down to earth.

"There's nothing as sexy as watching you come, *bébé*, from any angle." His gravelly voice rang with sincerity. "I need to feel you underneath me, today, to know you're mine. *Now*," he finished, making her quiver inside.

"*Yes*," she moaned, feeling suddenly so empty again that she was aching. With incredible strength that she could feel in the harsh planes of his muscles where they brushed her, he lifted her and carried her to the bed, letting her drop down onto the soft surface with a little bounce.

As she rolled fully onto her back, letting her thighs fall open in invitation, he stood over the bed like the Norman conqueror he often reminded her of, fresh from the heat of battle, returning to reclaim his woman. His face and stance were proud, in spite of his nudity, and his cock jutted from the silk mat of dark curls, thick and so swollen and hard that she could see the veins along the sides.

She made a wordless sound of appreciation and went more liquid. He smiled — a feral smile of pure lust.

"*Mine*," he grunted as he came over to her.

As she thrust into her with one long stroke, she gasped out her reply. "*Yours*," she answered, tightening all around him as he seated himself fully inside her, filling her completely.

"You're so tight, *chérie*." His voice again sounded strangled, and she tried to relax, but her sheath rippled around him.

"You just feel so good. Don't stop," she continued. "Need *you*." She knew she wasn't explaining well, but he seemed to understand. The feeling of him inside her had her right on the brink of coming again already.

"Whatever you need is yours," he answered, and drove into her again, starting a steady rhythm. After three long strokes, she tightened and shook with the pleasure of her release, which seemed to go on and on as he plunged into her relentlessly, every ridge of his thick cock dragging against the sensitive nerves inside her sheath so that she quivered and shuddered uncontrollably. The muscles of his arms, now sheened with sweat, looked like marble in the dim, golden light of the small lamp, and his expression was consumed with desire, but his eyes held something more. Something better. They were filled with pure love and commitment. Devotion. He was worshipping her, loving her with his entire body — with his entire self.

Even though she felt like her earlier pleasure had never really ebbed, when he began to thrust harder and reached to gently stroke one finger over her little bundle of nerves, the combined sensations sent her soaring up to a new level of arousal, of undiluted bliss, so that every muscle in her body clenched around him simultaneously then released until she became pure sensation. Love.

She gave a guttural cry and he rocked his hips, burying himself into her one last time then flooding her with jet after jet of hot liquid. She gasped with pleasure at every twitch and movement of his still-hard cock inside of her, her nerves and skin oversensitive from the extreme heights of pleasure. He finally collapsed on top of her and she clutched his weight and bulk with her arms and her legs, reveling in a deep feeling of possession. She kissed his shoulder, tasting the spicy salt of his sweat, too boneless with satisfaction to even try to touch or kiss him anywhere else. They lay together like that for long moments, the only sound their harsh breathing, until he finally managed to semi-roll off her with a groan of pure contentment. He trailed his fingers up and down her side in a tender gesture that made her shiver.

"I think you might have just killed me," she laughed, drawing a deep breath, the first since he'd been crushing her deliciously. "Instead of death by a thousand cuts, death by a thousand orgasms."

Pierre's snort was amused. "This *is* how I always pictured heaven," he answered, only opening one eye, his half-smile wicked. "Or at least, since I met you and you almost sat on my lap."

"I didn't know you were there," she protested laughingly.

"Alas, I felt I had to be a gentleman and announce my presence. An impulse I have regretted ever since."

Her answering laughter felt like it bubbled up from deep inside her, from some new well of joy. She turned a little bit more to her side so she could see him better, and when she did, the deep love she saw reflected in his eyes made her suck in a soft breath.

"You got the girl, didn't you?" she asked, and feathered a kiss on his chest.

"You make a good point, *bébé*. I'm the luckiest damn asshole out there and I should show you my appreciation that you would take a chance on me every single day, by inviting you to sit on my lap."

Her surprised bark of laughter was loud in the silent house, and she swatted him without heat. "You're incorrigible."

"I made you laugh, didn't I?" he challenged.

"*Touché*, Monsieur Gaspard. You are a funny, sexy bastard," she teased, and snuggled closer into the heat of his body, feeling a now-familiar heat rising inside her at his touch.

"*Ah-ah, non, chérie*," he countered. "I'm *your* funny, sexy bastard now."

"Yes, you are," she agreed, and pointed to her mouth for his kiss.

Want to see more from this author? Here's a taster for you to enjoy!

The Au Pair and the Beast
Aurora Russell

Excerpt

"Wait... He's sending his own car and *driver* to pick you up from the train station? And take you to his *castle*? How deliciously Gothic! It's probably set high up on some cliffs, overlooking an impossibly picturesque view of waves crashing onto the rocks."

Veronica quirked her lips into a smile at Katrin's words as they crackled through her cell phone, the reception seeming to go in and out as she rode along. Her best friend had a pronounced flair for the dramatic, which had only been enhanced by a number of drama classes in college.

"Well, when you put it that way...it *does* sound pretty glamorous," she laughingly agreed. "If it looks anything like that, I'll definitely text a picture of the view, complete with fog and sea spray."

Her friend's answering chuckle was amused. "How does Madame Montreaux know this guy again?"

Thinking back on it, Veronica wasn't sure the woman who led her French conversation group had ever actually told her...not specifically, anyway. "Weird. I'm not really sure... She just pulled me aside after our group one day and mentioned she'd heard about a job she thought I might be perfect for, you know, since she knew I'd lost my job when Dumfries & Partners was acquired. I got the impression—maybe just from her voice or something?—that he's some sort of family friend, but she was super skimpy on details." She drummed her fingers on her armrest as she considered. "I had to sign a confidentiality agreement before they even sent me the job description."

"Hmm-m." The one short word seemed filled with both skepticism and suspicion. "How old are the kids?"

"Just one child. A boy. I think he's four... Not in school yet, but he goes to preschool."

Veronica watched as the increasingly rural and wooded landscape flew by outside the window. The day was gray and dreary, but the beauty of the wilds of Maine was still undeniable. The well-modulated, incongruously feminine automated voice of the announcer came over the loudspeakers.

"Next stop, Grant's Cliff. Grant's Cliff is a flagged stop. Please notify the conductor if you are getting off at this stop."

Excitement and nerves combined into one powerful spark that set off a flurry of butterflies in Veronica's stomach, even as she stood and started to gather up her things.

"Sorry, K... Gotta go. They just called my stop. Call you later, okay?"

"Yes! Call, text, everything... I'll be waiting impatiently to hear that you haven't been chained up in this guy's basement—or dungeon. Whatever. Be careful! And good luck!"

Cradling the phone between her shoulder and cheek as she reached for her bag from the overhead storage, Veronica barked a laugh, and it was muffled. "Thank you?"

"Anytime! Bye!"

"Bye," Veronica answered, letting her bag drop into the seat and clicking to end the call on her phone. And it seemed it wasn't a moment too soon as she caught the conductor's eye and the train began to slow. She'd told him earlier where she was getting off and she was glad she had, since it didn't look like anyone else on the train was making a move to leave. Grant's Cliff was apparently not a popular destination.

"Right this way, miss." The conductor's weathered face creased into a kindly smile as he motioned her with one work-hardened hand.

"Thanks." She gave an answering grin and slipped the strap of her suitcase over her shoulder crosswise, sliding it to her back so she could hurry down the center aisle more easily. "Am I the only one getting off?"

"A-yup," he said, his Maine accent plain. She thought that was all he'd say, but as she stepped out of the open door onto the small platform, she heard him add, "Not much out here nowadays, apart from the castle and the beast."

Startled, she turned back, but the doors had already swished closed and the train began to pull away. *Okay then.*

She turned back and surveyed the deserted station. It was really more of a booth set next to a concrete slab platform with steps leading up to it. The metal sign for the station name was no bigger than a street sign and looked weathered. The dreary day had given way to fog, and now that the train had left, the only sound was the muffled rustling of the wind through thousands of trees. *Where the heck is the driver?* she wondered. Even as she looked around, half of her mind was still on the conductor's strange words. *What did he mean by the beast? Why hasn't anyone else mentioned it? Is this, like, a hotspot for sasquatch hunters? Or the home of a rogue grizzly? Wait! Are there even grizzly bears in Maine?* She thought maybe there were only black bears. But still, a rogue black bear could definitely be a beast.

When someone's gentle hand touched her shoulder, pulling her from her thoughts, she screeched and jumped what felt like three feet off the ground.

"Mademoiselle Carson? Veronica Carson?" The middle-aged man's accent was unmistakably French, and he pronounced her first name as *Vehr-oh-nee-ka*. She quickly raised her hand to her neck where her pulse was still racing.

"Yes," she nodded, a little breathless. "So sorry. I didn't hear anyone."

The man, who she noticed now was wearing a dark suit and even a driver's hat, smiled understandingly. "The fog. When it is thick like this, well…everything is hushed."

"Of course, that makes sense." She was relieved at such a simple explanation.

He held out his hand formally. "Claude Hormet, in service to Monsieur Reynard for many years."

She held her hand to meet his, and it was immediately taken into a firm handshake. "Nice to meet you, Monsieur Hormet."

His smile widened at her pronunciation of his name, and she thought she saw surprise flicker in his eyes. "It's a pleasure to meet you as well, Mademoiselle. We were told you spoke French well, and I can already hear it, if you don't mind my saying so."

"Thank you. That's very kind of you. I'm happy to switch over if you'd like, so you can really hear me."

Monsieur Hormet smiled again. "I would enjoy that, but later. For now, I will escort you to the château."

He took her bag from her and led her to a shiny, black Lincoln sedan that looked pristine in spite of the fact that it must have been at least thirty years old. He opened the back door, and once she'd slid onto the back seat, he gave a little bow before closing the door behind her. She didn't even hear the trunk close after he'd put her suitcase in, and when they began to move, the ride was so smooth that it felt like they were floating.

Monsieur Hormet didn't speak again, and sensing that it would possibly be considered too informal for her to initiate conversation, Veronica maintained silence as well. Instead, she took out her folder with a copy of her resume and list of references. She reviewed her notes again, but they were sparse. From the barebones details that had accompanied the job description, she really didn't know a lot about the open position and still didn't know anything more about her prospective employer than his last name, so she rehearsed again in her head what she could say about her experience.

She was so deep in thought, comfortable on the sumptuous leather of the seats, that she didn't really look up until the car began to slow. Then...*wow*. The mansion that loomed before her was truly a castle, made of stone with towers and turrets. If it had had a moat and not located in Maine, she would not have been surprised if someone had told her it was from the Middle Ages.

She must have made some sort of sound because Monsieur Hormet caught her gaze in the rearview mirror.

"Ah, the château is beautiful, no?"

Looking back at the lines of the massive structure, Veronica noticed that they were surprisingly delicate as well. Large it might be, but this was also a masterpiece of artistry, balanced and elegant. Still trying to look at every part of the castle at the same time, she answered with enthusiasm, "Oh yes, absolutely gorgeous!"

They pulled up right to the front steps, and Monsieur Hormet came around to help her out of the car. The air that buffeted her face was cooler than at the train station, damp and heavy, carrying the unmistakable salty tang of the ocean. She curved her lips into a small smile when she heard the distant crash of waves on something. Katrin was going to be overjoyed that her guess had to be at least partly correct.

"If you'll follow me, Mademoiselle, I'll show you to the large salon." Monsieur Hormet glanced at the front windows and nodded slightly at some small movement inside. "Eveline will let Monsieur Reynard know you've arrived."

Still craning her neck as discreetly as possible to see everything at once, Veronica followed him up a large number of stone steps and into the château. She had only a glimpse of the enormous entry hall before they went down a spacious hallway into a room that looked like some sort of formal parlor. There were several seating areas around the room, and he motioned for her to sit in a straight-backed armchair in the cluster nearest to the windows. Even with the fog, she could still tell that the windows here overlooked the ocean. A gray-green expanse of icy-cold Atlantic water, the view looked imposing rather than inviting. She loved it.

Fighting the urge to press her nose to the glass of the windowpanes, she sat down on the chair instead in what she hoped was a professional, dignified manner. She took out the folder once again and waited. An ornate gilded clock, which looked like an antique that would have been at home in the art museum in Boston, ticked, and the sound was loud in the otherwise-silent room. At the *snick* of the door handle turning, she leaped to her feet and turned to greet her interviewer. The figure that entered was considerably shorter and faster than she'd expected, though.

As he barreled toward her at full tilt, Veronica saw that the little boy had a mass of golden-blond hair, bright blue eyes and cheeks that glowed pink with good health. His happy face was dominated by a huge grin. She braced for possible impact, but he stopped abruptly right in front of her and eyed her curiously.

"You're pretty," he said in French, "but I don't like your coat. I'm not supposed to say 'hate' or 'ugly'." He looked up at her expectantly.

Veronica stifled a laugh as she darted a glance down at her suit coat. It was something she'd bought for interviews, and she internally agreed that it wasn't the most attractive thing she owned—more about practicality than fashion. But still…

"It sounds like you're doing a good job listening, then," she answered in French, skirting around the question. She set her folder, which she'd still been clutching, on the seat of the chair and crouched down so she was eye-level with the boy. "What's your name? Mine is Veronica."

"Jean-Philippe. Yvette says you're here to take care of me, but only if Papa likes you. I don't have a *maman*. She died. Our dog died too. Sometimes I get sad and cry and Papa says that's okay." Veronica's heart clenched at the childish words, but she fought another laugh at what he said next. "Did you bring a present? Papa always brings a present and hides it in one of his pockets. *Oncle* Marius too. Is that why you're wearing that coat, to hide presents?" He eyed her outfit with more enthusiasm.

"It's a pleasure to meet you, Jean-Philippe," she answered, then shook her head regretfully. "I didn't know, so no presents today, but I promise that if I stay, I'll bring you something next time I go into town. How's that?"

He bobbed his little head as he nodded, making his fine blond hair glint, even in the dim sunlight from the gloomy day. "That sounds good," he agreed. "I hope you go to town soon."

She couldn't have hidden her smile this time if she'd tried, so she didn't bother. Another noise made her look up again, toward the door, where a young woman stood, looking a bit harried. Her chest rose and fell rapidly, as if she'd been running. She wore some sort of uniform dress, not black-and-white but something about it made Veronica think she might be a maid or housekeeper. Her look at Jean-Philippe was a mix of exasperation and affection.

The man who entered on her heels, though, made Veronica shoot to her feet and straighten her back. He was tall, probably close to six-and-a-half feet, and his shoulders and chest were broad and muscular. He wore a suit that must have been custom-tailored to fit his large frame so perfectly, and he exuded an air of pure power. Confidence. She would have had to be blind or utterly oblivious not to feel an awareness of such a man.

Where his frame and his very presence seemed to fill the room, it was his face that really captivated her. Dark, wavy hair framed the most attractive face she thought she'd ever seen. He wasn't what she would call handsome—his Roman nose was just a little too prominent—but his features were masculine, strong and absolutely stunning. His eyes, which she could tell even from this distance were a deep brown like melted dark chocolate and framed with thick dark lashes, seemed to see all the way into her from across the room. She felt goosebumps rise on her arms and up her neck, and she couldn't seem to tear her own gaze away.

When he started to move, whatever spell that was keeping her silent was broken. To her surprise, she noticed that he walked with a cane in steps that looked like they carefully concealed pain.

"Oh, Monsieur, I'm so sorry. He got away from me when he was supposed to be following me," the young woman apologized to the man who she guessed must be Monsieur Reynard.

He inclined his head slightly, and although his face remained impassive, Veronica somehow got the impression of tolerance.

"I understand, Yvette. You may return to your regular duties." His voice was deep and rumbling, full of gravel. It rolled through the quiet room, filling every corner, though he spoke quietly.

The young woman gave a little bow and hurried from the room gratefully, leaving only Veronica, Jean-Philippe and Monsieur Reynard.

"Papa!" the little boy exclaimed, confirming Veronica's guess at the identity of the man. She saw him grimace almost imperceptibly as his little boy crashed into his leg in a show of preschool affection.

"I see you've met Miss Carson, my son," he said, looking at Veronica as he tousled the baby-fine mop of hair.

"Oh yes! Do you like her? Is she staying?"

The question fell heavily in the quiet room, and Veronica turned to pick up the folder again.

"I brought a copy of my resume and a list of references —"

"No need." Monsieur Reynard interrupted her, gesturing with his hand as if to wave her words away. "I've seen enough. The job is yours."

Veronica's mouth fell open. "I, uh… We just met."

He raised his dark eyebrows. "So we did."

She shook her head. Why was he making her so unsettled? Good Heavens, she was usually more articulate than this! "I mean, you haven't interviewed me. Don't you want to know…more?"

He shrugged and inclined his head to one side. "Mademoiselle, I'm known for being a good judge of character, with very few exceptions. It's part of what has made me so successful. Jean-Philippe needs someone who is good with children, experienced and speaks French. From what I heard, you are all of these things."

Veronica felt a warm flush rising up her neck, straight to her cheeks then right on up to her hairline. For some reason, the idea of not being aware of *this* man, with his outsize presence, made her beyond flustered. "You were listening?" she asked in a voice that was, she congratulated herself, almost normal.

He shrugged in a wonderfully Mediterranean way. "Not on purpose, but the door was cracked open and sound carries down the hallway."

Mentally replaying her conversation with Jean-Philippe, Veronica couldn't figure out what she could possibly have said to warrant this instant acceptance. "And I said enough to give you such confidence?"

She thought she had gotten over her initial shock of awareness at how very handsome he was, like someone jumping into cold water who starts acclimating. She was wrong. When he turned the full force of his dark, soulful eyes on her and turned up the corners of his mouth in what might have been the beginnings of a smile, she nearly had to catch her breath. She felt the goosebumps rise again all over her arms.

"You did pass the background check with flying colors, and you must know your accent is beautiful. But mostly, you didn't miss a beat when my son insulted your er…ensemble." He motioned tactfully to her suit and she opened her mouth in indignation, only to snap it shut at his next words. "I truly believe you to be a young woman of good sense, patience and kindness. Those are qualities I value beyond all others."

His praise warmed her and was so close to describing the kind of person she hoped she was that she felt like another piece clicked into the odd connection she might be starting to feel with him.

"Thank you. In that case, I accept the position." He didn't return her smile, but she thought maybe his eyes crinkled the slightest bit at the corners.

"I'll have Monsieur Hormet bring in the paperwork. Come along, Jean-Phillipe," he said, turning and making his slow, deliberate way to the door with a gait she suspected concealed very-well-hidden pain. Jean-Philippe overtook him to sprint out of the door before his father.

All in all, Veronica was feeling pretty darn satisfied and relieved at avoiding the stress of a real interview when she heard Monsieur Reynard's last words before he left the room.

"Such a relief to meet a young woman who doesn't trouble herself too much over her clothes."

Home of Erotic Romance

Sign up for our newsletter and find out about all our romance book releases, eBook sales and promotions, sneak peeks and FREE romance books!

About the Author

Aurora is originally from the frozen tundra of the upper-Midwest (ok, not frozen all the time!) but now loves living in New England with her real-life hero/husband, two wonderfully silly sons, and one of the most extraordinary cats she has ever had the pleasure to meet. But she still goes back to the Midwest to visit, just never in January.

She doesn't remember a time that she didn't love to read, and has been writing stories since she learned how to hold a pencil. She has always liked the romantic scenes best in every book, story, and movie, so one day she decided to try her hand at writing her own romantic fiction, which changed her life in all the best ways.

Aurora loves to hear from readers. You can find her contact information, website details and author profile page at https://www.totallybound.com